CROWNKEEPER

✦ BOOK TWO ✦

ANNE WHEELER

For Mom, who wanted more.

IRAELA
NARCIENNE
CRESQUET RIVER
MENCOTE DESE
KINGDOM of MEIRDRE
N
NAVASIAN

NANTOISE
GALVAN OCEAN
CHARMONT RIVER
VISTEL
LOCHFIELD CASTLE
ARSELE FOREST
HASZEN
ELTERNOW
THE MOORS
KALCINE RIVER
HARNOW
BRANNITZ
ILLRUS RIVER
EDRISTA OUTPOST

CHAPTER ONE

Today, the map was quiet.

I circled the ballroom once more, my feet trampling the map inlaid on the floor, pretending to practice a waltz with a non-existent partner. In truth, I was eyeing the mahogany borders and oak cities and pine mountains beneath my silk shoes, searching for any indication my kingdom was in trouble. I'd been born one of those exceptional children, gifted with the connection to the kingdom, and the map—it spoke to me and had since I'd put that cursed crown on my head during my betrothal period. It showed me Meirdre's misfortunes, as it showed every crownkeeper.

But married now, if not Queen of Meirdre, I'd quickly grown used to the strangeness of my power since arriving at Lochfeld Castle. I joked to myself that my ability to see the map's sparkles and shimmers that warned of danger was bizarre enough to make my other situation—that of a peasant girl yanked from her home and brought to a castle to marry a king she'd never before seen—not *quite* so odd. Not that I'd forgotten Mama and Papa in the least, but the much-needed comfort secured for them by my marriage had a way of softening homesickness. They had coin and several healthy head of cattle, and I had . . . well, warmth and fine dresses, if not love.

My gaze swept from the far western border, out past the Tourmel Mountains, then all the way back to Lochfeld where I stood, and then, finally, to my erstwhile hometown of Elternow. I'd worried about Elternow incessantly when I'd first arrived, even more than the sovereign's castle. But the wood throughout the kingdom remained glossy and dark, not sparkling and glowing, so I lowered my arms and settled into a chair by the window for a short break. Anyone who looked inside would see me a fool, constantly dancing with myself, and I needed to be seen as anything but a fool here, in King Laurent's court.

Though to tell the truth, I felt a bit like one today, even as I rested and my breathing became regular. Not much sun shone through the thick, impenetrable glass today, and no one danced in a dark ballroom, especially without a partner. The spring rains of central Meirdre hadn't quite moved on, and heavy clouds hung above the castle towers. The dreary weather wouldn't normally affect my mood—a farmer's daughter never cursed the arrival of the light showers that followed our harsh winters, naturally—but here in the castle, it was another story. I needed the happiness of the sun. Silk gowns and sufficient food or not, the sunlight was my only happiness some days. With a sigh, I tucked a stray piece of hair behind my ear and searched for the very slightest hint of a sunbeam that might lift my mood.

There was none, so I looked back at the map. From my position at the window I could see the entirety of the kingdom—no waltz about the expansive space required—but the king had been the one to place the chair here, so I objected to using it more than necessary. It turned out that being married to a man who didn't love you made having certain principles easy. Besides, my dancing skills were much improved after practicing hour after hour.

It wasn't as though the king helped with my waltz skills, either—not that I especially wanted him to. I'd have to dance with him eventually, I knew, and the idea made my hands clench into fists. Thank the heavens Lochfeld wasn't known for its social engagements and galas. At least, not anymore. The castle was almost empty except for the king, myself, his sister and her husband, and the bare minimum of servants. Courtiers and advisors were rare, unless they had a reason to be here.

As the memory of dancing with the king at our betrothal ball floated into my mind, the faintest glimmer of light caught my eye, and I leaned forward, trying to shove the memory aside. He'd almost kissed me that night—had touched my hand, anyway—and I'd take any distraction to dispel the heat that suddenly flashed in my cheeks. King Laurent could not be allowed to affect me like that. Not after what he'd done to me.

I blinked away his memory. Once more, it was Harnow that had caught my attention, sparkling like a diamond. They'd had an outbreak of measles months before—in fact, the very same outbreak that had proven my map reading ability to the king, the crisis that had confirmed me a crownkeeper. After the way the king had treated me then, I didn't like to think of either the measles or Harnow. I was certain that for the rest of my life I would connect the small town with my wedding night. Not the wedding night of most queens of Meirdre, I'd spent it lying awake next to my bridegroom, tears in my eyes as the wounds from the whip had pulled at the skin on my back. The only thing that brought me some relief was the remembrance that the king hadn't slept well, either.

But I had a job to do, as distasteful as it sometimes—most of the time—could be. With a short glance at the door for any witnesses, I crept up to the miniature house inlaid on the floor, the mark that symbolized Harnow. Still cautious of the power I'd been granted, I knelt to look closer. Yes, Harnow, shimmering like a rainbow washed in rose, was definitely in trouble.

But what kind of trouble, I had no way of knowing.

There had to be some kind of pattern to the flashes and colors the map in the floor radiated, but so far, I hadn't figured it out. The last time Harnow had made its problem known, it had been white, like diamonds. Today it was still white, but there was something odd about it—small rosy flashes in the glittering map symbol. I mentally marked the image to add to my journal later, then shrugged it off. Likely colors meant nothing. Just one more oddity the Creator had bestowed on the map. But with time, and luck, and meticulous recordkeeping, I'd be able to determine if there was a pattern. It wasn't as though I had much else to do. No baking, no escorting the cow to the pasture, no climbing trees. No acting as a lookout for rebels who turned out to be anything but.

Regardless, the king would need to be informed.

Standing, I ran my hands over my gown and checked my image in the mirror. Sara, becoming a friend more than a servant, had chosen something a little more velvet than the balmy yet dreary weather had called for, but King Laurent would appreciate that I looked like I'd made an effort, and one of the things I *did* focus on these days was avoiding his cutting comments about my looks. My hair wasn't quite as elegant as the dress, but perhaps he wouldn't notice. I prayed he wouldn't notice.

That risky decision made, I headed to the king's private office. The ability to see him there instead of the throne room was a benefit of my marriage that I hadn't expected, but quite appreciated. His Majesty in the throne room was the tyrant who'd sentenced me to death; King Laurent in his office was the civil administrator who dealt in paperwork and coinage. Bothersome, yes, but not a threat. At least, that was what I had convinced myself.

A sentry nodded at my approach and reached for the door. I steeled my back, preparing for yet another disagreeable conversation once he opened it. Conversations with the king, if not always brief like I preferred, were always unpleasant. Had been ever since our wedding in Lochfeld's dungeon.

"Her Grace, sire."

I tiptoed inside at the introduction and curtsied in front of the king's antique desk before meeting his gaze. At first, he was barely visible behind the stacks of parchment and other books, though it wasn't quite as disorganized as my imagination wanted, and he shoved a few aside, clearing my view completely as I straightened. Dark circles surrounded azure eyes in his face, and I looked away for an instant, toward the window that overlooked what had once been the bailey. He had no right to be exhausted. If anyone slept well at night, it was the imperturbable King Laurent of Meirdre, who never deigned to trouble himself with the plights of his subjects.

"Yes, my dear?" he asked, evening the stack of paper to his right without giving it so much as a glance. "Something is happening?"

Of course something was happening. We didn't speak otherwise. Yes, sometimes we ate together, but we never conversed, sometimes we even shared a bed to fool the servants into thinking our marriage was solid, though we never touched or even spoke when that happened. Our sole verbal interaction—truly our sole interaction beyond painstakingly avoiding and ignoring each other—was when I informed him of trouble. Sometimes I wondered if he'd rather not speak to me even then. What would he do if I sent a written message with a servant or one of the royal guards?

I decided I'd find out next time.

Maybe.

"It's Harnow, sire," I said, clasping my hands in front of me and giving him an even, small smile. Not a happy one, because I didn't want to encourage him or seem foolish, but a frown implied . . . the wrong things. What wrong things, I wasn't exactly sure. "It's glowing again."

The word *again* was a mistake, but it came without warning from my subconscious. Perhaps his affectionate form of address had rankled me more than I'd appreciated. The use of *Her Grace* certainly had, and it wasn't because I had any desire to be queen. The desire to be respected and loved, yes, I had that, but that simply wasn't King Laurent, and there was no use hoping for something that would never happen. At least, that was what I told myself. What woman didn't want her husband to value and admire her as something more than a tool to keep his power secure?

"Hmm." The king set down his pen, folded his hands in front of him, and stared at me over the desk. "Harnow again. What do you think is the problem there? You've spent so much time watching the map since arriving at Lochfeld—you must have some idea."

"I—" I shut my mouth and frowned. This was new. He'd never asked for my opinion before, simply acknowledged my information and dismissed me with an offhand wave. "I have no idea. Perhaps the outbreak isn't over."

"Hmm," he repeated. "That would be . . . unfortunate."

Unfortunate? What kind of response was that? I shifted to my opposite leg and switched my hands behind my back, frantic for his dismissal. Since my other reports had been met with indifference—though each one was investigated, I was sure—I hadn't planned on standing in front of him for so long.

And that was a problem, for the longer I did, the more chance for him to comment on my hair, messily braided in a style I knew he disliked. But the map had shown me a dust storm in the Mencote Desert just last week, and though I knew the map didn't keep any kind of a set schedule, I'd never thought something else would be happening so soon after that storm. If I had, I would have made certain to be more presentable.

Then again, why should I have bothered impressing the king with my looks? Many women had and did, I knew—I saw the looks of the daughters of nobles who visited, even after our marriage—but since he and I scarcely spoke, I didn't see it as a priority. He might be my king, yes, and I afforded him the grudging respect his position demanded, but he wasn't truly my husband.

Not when I didn't love him.

Not when he'd punished my childhood friend by proxy—with my body and a whip.

Not when he'd refused to give me the title of queen.

Not when—and we hid this secret from the entire court—we were husband and wife in name only.

When I didn't reply to his comment about a measles outbreak with the possibility of killing dozens as being *unfortunate*, the king broke his gaze and began to shuffle and restack some of the paper in front of him. Had I actually succeeded in making him uncomfortable? Just by standing here thinking to myself? It was something to remember for the next time. Anything that made him feel awkward meant I'd won a little something, and in the strange new world I currently inhabited, that was never something to discount.

"I will send out scouts," he said, as I began to wonder if he'd notice if I simply walked out. "Hopefully it's nothing, but . . . the map is so rarely wrong that we shouldn't begin to ignore it now."

"Thank you, sire. I'm sure the people of Harnow will be grateful for whatever help their liege is willing to provide." That flattery complete, I took a deep breath. "May I go?"

His eyes landed on my hair, and I clenched my fingers even tighter, daring him to say something about the curl that had somehow managed to escape and was hanging across my forehead. He picked up his pen and shifted a document in front of him.

"Yes," he replied, without looking up. "But next time, my dear, have Sara do your hair."

CHAPTER TWO

The single best thing about living in a castle, besides the sumptuous gowns I was rapidly becoming used to, was having unfettered access to a better-quality horse than I'd enjoyed at home, a horse meant simply for pleasure riding, not farm work. The one which had stolen my heart was the brindled mare who whinnied when I appeared in the stables and nuzzled at my hand when I approached. She made an acceptable replacement to the mare I'd been forced to leave when I'd arrived at Lochfeld Castle to marry the king, and I was grateful for her affection as I edged into her stall one gray spring afternoon.

As the lone stable boy saddled Skylark, I tried to ignore the fact I hadn't seen my husband in almost a week—the day after I'd informed him of Harnow's newest difficulties. He'd appeared in Lochfeld's chapel for a private liturgy that morning, given me a quick nod as I stared in surprise at his appearance, then disappeared to his rooms once more. I dared not intrude on whatever solitude he wanted, but there was a small part of my soul that resented the distance. He had hurt me, he had insulted me, and he dared treat me like I was something to discard? If anyone had implied that, it should have been me.

My skirts whipped around my ankles as I urged Skylark away from the castle. Not down the trail that led to the cliffs and then onward toward my hometown of Elternow, but north, across the open field that sat atop the mountain. The flat ground allowed a gallop, allowed me to breathe in the chill that still clung to the hills in places. Outside was the only place I could breathe these days. There was no royal guard directly at my back—though two sets of hoofbeats followed somewhere behind me, publicizing their distant existence—no Juliana, questioning why her brother and I seemed so aloof on the rare occasions we were together, and no memories. Not of my past life in Elternow, not of the emotions I'd thought I'd felt for Thomas, and not of my punishment at the king's command.

The broad meadow gave way to a line of trees ahead,

and I slowed Skylark to a canter. She tossed her head, irritated at how quickly I'd ended her run, but my legs were aching, and the forest was calling to me. I wouldn't run her through the stumps and roots, though, so I muttered a few reassuring words under my breath and guided her toward the narrow trail that led within. We could gallop back to Lochfeld later, but right now I needed to enjoy the beauty of nature at a speed that allowed me to see it.

My guards hung back the appropriate distance as the cloudy afternoon became even dimmer in the heavy cover of limbs and leaves. Shadows cast their gloom across my path, but it didn't bother me in any way that truly mattered. Even in spring this wood was thick enough to block most of the sun, which was why the trail led this way, I'd been told. The castle might be cool enough to bear when summer eventually arrived, Juliana said, but the spring a five-minute ride from where I sat was even cooler.

Skylark tossed her head and whinnied again, making her displeasure at the cancelled run evident. I ignored her and guided her farther inside, indulging in the sensation of freedom I'd thought I'd lost when I'd first come to Lochfeld. Right now, there were no servants, no king, no map, no responsibilities, no reminders of how I'd failed myself and my own desires. Just the distant hoofbeats of my guards, and they wouldn't dare interrupt my private afternoon.

I spun backward in the saddle as the whinnies and hoofbeats of more than one horse grew louder, but I couldn't see any riders. Were my guards so distant? The trail had turned though, heading west, so perhaps they were behind me on a curve. No matter. Nothing would ruin this ride, even if Skylark was less than thrilled about the change in plans.

I twisted forward again to continue deeper into the woods, then screamed as a figure smiled at me from one of the deeper shadows. My heart threatened to explode, then settled again. It was Captain Willem who sat astride his horse in the middle of the trail, his hands folded on the saddle in front of him and a wry expression on his face.

"You ought to be paying more attention to where you're headed, Your Grace."

I swallowed down the remainder of my abandoned scream and gave him a baleful glare. The captain of the royal guard knew he'd snuck up on me, had probably planned it once he'd heard Skylark coming down the trail, but he'd never apologize. That wasn't worth arguing about though because his very presence here could mean only one thing.

The king was somewhere deeper in the forest.

"And you could have made your presence known," I said, as steadily as I could. Willem wasn't the issue. And he couldn't know I was becoming distraught at the idea of encountering his master. That was King Laurent's order—no one could know how much we hated each other. I wondered if he honestly believed it was that much of a secret.

"It's hard to hide a horse on dry earth in the forest," he replied, "especially the way the wind is making everything echo today. If you were not paying attention to your surroundings, Your Grace, that is your fault and your fault alone. Perhaps more education in your own security is in order. We'll work on your knife skills tomorrow. And the next day as well, if I don't feel you've improved enough."

My mouth fell open at his reprimand. He was right, of course, and my security was something I couldn't ever take for granted now that I'd married the king, but what woman wanted a lecture?

Captain Willem shrugged as I sat there silent and motionless, then guided his mount around me. Turning around and following him back to Lochfeld would have been the prudent decision, but before I could, his royal charge trotted up to us on Foxfire, the stallion who hated me almost as much as his master did.

Trapped and silent, I clenched my jaw as the rest of the royal guard trailed him.

King Laurent pulled Foxfire to a stop and looked me up and down, somehow both expressionless and mocking, a paradox only a few men in the kingdom could manage.

"Out for a ride, my dear?" he asked. "It certainly is a pleasant day for it."

What tripe. Through the trees, the clouds were suddenly gathering above us, and if I wasn't mistaken, a raindrop had just landed on my head.

I lifted my chin and tried to relax my jaw. "Yes, sire. I've been enjoying it."

The king's gaze dropped to his hands, wound oddly tight in the reins. "Willem," he said to his nails, his tone sharp. "I will escort her back. The rest of you are dismissed for the remainder of the day."

"But I don't want to go back!" My protest surprised me as much as his appearance had.

He watched the rest of the guard head out of the forest before speaking again. "I would think you'd have learned by now that your desires are rather low in importance, all things considered."

His tone wasn't unfamiliar, but I stiffened my spine at the distaste in his comment. He couldn't even pretend to be civil to me now, even after he'd pretended in front of Captain Willem and the others? The disparity was disheartening.

"And I've also learned that I'm allowed an afternoon ride," I retorted.

Or had he changed his mind about how much freedom I was allowed?

"Not today." The king turned Foxfire toward the castle and nodded at me to follow, like I was an old hunting dog. "You need to check the map. Something might be happening, and I won't have you miss it because you were rambling around the woods."

Skylark moved to follow her stablemate. I yanked on the reins—harder than I'd intended—to stop her. "I checked this morning. There was nothing."

King Laurent stopped, then twisted slowly in his saddle as if he couldn't believe I'd refused his order. "Things may have changed since you were last there."

"They may have, but you can't possibly expect me to sit in the ballroom all day, every day, sire!"

Or maybe he could. After all, he'd married me because I had the power to see those dangers, and I'd agreed because I needed to protect my kingdom along with my own small family. I was an effective prisoner now, but I didn't need to be treated like one, did I? Couldn't I go for an afternoon ride? The magic was so particular that I believed the map would call to me if I was needed. The king didn't know that part of it, and although I wasn't certain, I was confident enough in the magic to risk a ride.

"I'm not expecting you to sit in the ballroom all day, every day. But as I said, things may have changed."

I opened my mouth to argue, then stopped as a flush crept up my neck. I hadn't lied, not exactly, but forgetful was as bad as falsehood when a kingdom's security was at stake, wasn't it? Or maybe it was King Laurent's fault for making the days all blend together into one.

He was still glaring at me from astride Foxfire, but I had to admit that he wasn't an unattractive man, especially seated on a powerful horse, his sword hanging at his side. He'd lost a bit of weight since winter, and though he could scarcely afford the loss, it had somehow emphasized the curve of his calves through his fitted breeches. Flushing, my gaze moved upward.

"What are you staring at, Riette, dear?"

I gasped at his question and brushed my hair back. How long had I been staring at those thick lashes and azure eyes?

"Nothing," I stammered. "Nothing."

"Really."

It wasn't a question that time, and my flush grew deeper. "I'm tired. Were you saying something?"

His eyebrows rose. "I was telling you that you're

needed back at Lochfeld. But if you're so exhausted, perhaps a casual ride through the grove would be better for you. Everyone deserves some rest, and the fresh air might do much to aid your fatigue. Maybe I've asked too much from you, after all."

I narrowed my eyes in return. It was like the king to offer me only enough to keep me content, but I was no fool. He had an ulterior motive today as well, though I had no idea what it was. Perhaps he simply didn't want to argue? Indifference was more his style than anger—and had been since our wedding.

"There's a spring," he added when I didn't reply. "I've just come from there, and I thought—"

"You thought what?" I demanded more rudely than I'd intended.

"I thought we could spend some time together while you rest."

"I do not require your presence in order to rest, sire."

The opposite, in fact.

"Yes, well . . ." He trailed off for a long while, and as a bird sang a rain song above us, my disloyal gaze fell to those calves once more. "That may be so. But I think I would enjoy your company today, and as my wife, I thought that perhaps—"

I didn't let him finish. I didn't need to in order to figure out what he was going to say. He wanted to spend time with me at long last, and that meant—that meant the cold distance between us might dwindle. It meant I might trust him, if not for the rest of my life, for a span of five long minutes.

And that couldn't happen. I wouldn't *let* it happen.

I dug my knees into Skylark's sides and bolted.

King Laurent didn't follow.

CHAPTER THREE

IF THE KING WAS SOMEONE I WANTED TO AVOID AS MUCH as possible, his sister, thank the heavens, was not. From my first day at Lochfeld, she'd made me feel welcome, and after my unusual marriage? She hadn't acted as though my relationship with her brother was anything other than normal, as if I hadn't come back to the castle a few weeks ago on Skylark at full speed, minutes before my husband, and then locked myself in my room all day. Perhaps that was because love didn't usually exist among royalty, but I suspected she was simply polite and kind enough to not bring attention to anything untoward. Whatever the reason, I loved her for it.

Today, as we relaxed in her parlor, the spring sun spilling through the narrow windows, I loved her even more for choosing a pastime that didn't put me in as much of a disadvantage as it could, given my upbringing. It was always possible she was letting me win on purpose, but her facial expressions, amusing and despondent at the same time, told another story. It was hard to believe a relative of the king lacked strategic skills, even in something as innocuous as chess, but Juliana had clearly focused her educational pursuits elsewhere. She wrinkled her nose at me as I moved my queen, and I grinned in return.

"Checkmate."

She toppled her ebony king with a light finger. "I don't believe I have much else to teach you. You're too fast a learner—and my chess skills are sorely lacking."

"Hardly. It took me almost a month to figure out how to beat you." Satisfied in my charity, I tucked my feet under me in the deep chair and arranged my skirts. Unladylike, yes, but we were alone in the parlor. A few days ago, she'd commented that her servants had become a burden and that she preferred the solitude of doing everything herself. It'd been a strange comment, but not one I could argue with. "At least I've been successful in learning something."

"You'll get there." Juliana eyed me critically. "I hear you've been spending quite a bit of time in the library, anyway. Soon you'll know more about Meirdrean history than Laurent."

She wasn't wrong about my time in the library. I could read, but my few years of schooling in Elternow seemed woefully inadequate now that I was married to her brother. Despite her poor chess skills, she could speak of things with more cleverness and grace than I could—science and history and politics. It was a good thing the castle was as empty of advisors and courtiers as it had been when I'd first arrived. I couldn't imagine having to show my ignorance in front of even more people. King Laurent was bad enough.

"It's quiet," I replied. "And I can read without anyone knowing I'm doing it."

"Laurent, you mean."

I nodded. Truly, I'd been hiding so he couldn't see me learn *anything*. History, writing, numbers, all of it. The shame of my husband knowing my math skills were limited to what I'd needed to know in order to sell milk and wheat rankled me. My confidence was growing as I learned more and more, but not quickly enough for me to feel I truly belonged at Lochfeld.

"Well," she went on while packing away the chess set, "there's no reason to be ashamed of it. I'm sure he knows your education was—"

"Your Grace!"

The door must have opened silently, for we both spun around at the interruption. Willem strode across the parlor, paler than I'd ever seen him. Juliana jumped to her feet, then as if she realized I should be the one to reply, lowered herself slowly back down.

"Yes?" I asked through gritted teeth. I wasn't exactly required to greet the king when he came home from wherever it was that he disappeared to, but things seemed to go better for a few days when I did. Sometimes I even received a smile from him. "I wasn't aware he had returned to Lochfeld."

"He's upstairs." Willem's voice shook. "Ill. Both of you need to stay away from that wing. Your Grace"—this was addressed to me, I assumed, since our rooms were next to each other—"I'll move your things. Is there anything specific you need for the next few weeks or so?"

"I— why do you need to move my things? How bad is he?" My chest tightened, and I couldn't understand why. Meirdre needed a king, and King Laurent had no heir, but someone would take his place. I shouldn't care what happened to him as a person.

"Measles," Willem replied. "We can't take the chance it'll spread to you."

I moved toward him in relief, while in the corner of

my eye, Juliana stood and retreated from the room —rapidly.

"I've had the measles," I said.

"Good. That's good. Do you mind?" His shoulders sank as he waved a hand at the nearest chair.

He looked exhausted, and I nodded as he fell into it. Juliana would have it burned, but I couldn't very well say no.

"But how did he contract the measles?" I asked. "Has someone else in the castle . . ."

I trailed off. We would have heard long before now if one of the few residents was ill. Was this related to wherever the king had disappeared?

My heart skipped a beat.

Harnow.

Had he ridden for Harnow himself the day after I'd encountered him in the forest? Part of me had wondered if King Laurent hadn't in fact left Lochfeld at all, that perhaps he'd been holed up somewhere in the castle these past weeks. Or maybe he'd gone on some scouting trip around the Nantolsen border. I really didn't know, and hadn't cared, beyond assuming he was gone. But then again, I hadn't had a compelling reason to look for him, even when he'd disappeared shortly after our ride.

Was his insistence on spending time with me in the woods

because he'd intended to ride for the stricken town shortly afterward?

"No." Willem folded his arms. "No one in the castle has it or has been exposed, and we must keep it that way. I shouldn't have brought him back, but—but he insisted. I'd thought him delirious enough with fever that I could convince him the camp we'd stopped in on the way back was Lochfeld, but I wasn't that lucky. He wants to die at home."

I gasped. Men like King Laurent didn't die. They lived forever to make their wives and kingdoms miserable.

"He's bad off, Your Grace. I wouldn't expect a miracle."

Time stood still as I rose to my feet, and my loathing for my husband cracked. I could feel it somewhere deep in my soul, like the glass in our house in Elternow had shattered that one night. Had I brought this upon him with my refusal to forgive him? That wasn't how life worked, but I couldn't shake the feeling this was my fault. But it wasn't as if I had sent him to Harnow.

"Then I want to see him," I replied quietly. "Right now."

Willem's brows drew together—no doubt he was well-aware of how little the king and I cared for each other—but he nodded and motioned me into the corridor. I kept up with his stride, long, yes, but slow from exhaustion, as we climbed the stairs to the wing in which Laurent and I had rooms. Two servants were heading in the opposite direction, their expressions grim. Were they gathering supplies for their return, or was I the only one in the entire castle who wasn't susceptible to the disease? The sudden weight of responsibility fell on me like an entire haystack as I peered into his room.

The window was open, and the heavy velvet drapes blew in the spring breeze, though someone had tried to tie them shut. The sun had moved on past this side of the castle, so it was hard to see the figure lying in bed, especially with the pervasive oil lamps extinguished and only a few candles for illumination. I clasped my hands to my sides to avoid lighting a few more. Laurent, if he had any senses left now, probably had a ruthless headache. It was one of the few things I remembered from my experience years ago.

"Riette." The tall figure on the other side of Laurent's canopied bed rose into the light and frowned. Father Gerritt's easy tenor and the cautious movements of his elderly body would always be familiar to me, but I could scarcely recognize him through the gloom. "You shouldn't be here. Go, now, and don't come back."

"You're certain it's measles?" I asked.

"Can't be mistaken for anything else, even by a novice." He nodded at Laurent's bare arms, covered in an angry red rash.

"Then it's fine." I slunk toward the bed, cringing inside. Tyrant and awful husband though Laurent might be, I, unlike Thomas, didn't necessarily want to see him dead. Just . . . away from me. I shouldn't have been fighting with this compassion I didn't understand. "We didn't have the luxury of avoiding disease in Elternow."

If Father Gerritt was offended by my comment, he didn't show it. "The king will be angry you were allowed in here, even immune—though I suppose he's not in any condition to find out now. Perhaps we can keep it our secret."

A chair appeared behind me, and I sank into it as Willem disappeared back into the corridor. While my eyes adjusted, the reason for his and Father Gerritt's alarm was obvious. Laurent hadn't brushed off the disease as I had, like most of the children in Elternow did. The raised rash covered every exposed area of his skin, and though his eyes were closed in what appeared to be a fitful sleep, he shook with the pain of a man wracked with fever. His nightclothes were damp, and the bedsheet pulled halfway over him, clean though it looked, was just as drenched.

"Yes," I murmured, reaching for Laurent's hand, for

reasons I'd never be able to explain. It was cold in mine, even with the fever. "I suppose we can."

"It'll have to do." Father Gerritt reached for a rag in a bowl of water, then sighed. "He didn't want you to know where he was or what he'd been doing. Said it wasn't any of your business, and he'd have the head of anyone who spoke of it to you. Thankfully, he's so out of it that I feel my head is quite safe."

"And he was where and doing what, exactly?" I asked as he ran the cloth across Laurent's head.

"Harnow." He peered at me in that peculiar way he had, like he could see into my mind. "Doing what he could for them during the outbreak."

I gave a sudden bark of laughter, only cutting myself off at his disapproving expression. Knowing Laurent had ridden for Harnow was one thing, but being told he'd done it out of his own kindness was something else entirely.

"I'm sorry, Father," I replied, "but His Majesty was not in Harnow tending to ill children."

He shrugged and wrung out the rag, unperturbed once more. Since I'd been at Lochfeld, I'd come to understand that nothing bothered him.

"Well, tending to ill children might be a bit of a stretch. But delivering supplies directly to homes and overseeing the hospital tent, yes. You can believe me or not," he said at my obvious distrust, leaning back in his own chair, "but I saw it with my own eyes."

I dropped Laurent's motionless hand and stared at the priest. I'd been so caught up with Juliana and chess and Skylark and the joys of spring that I hadn't noticed Father Gerritt had been away from the palace along with Laurent. And truthfully, his library was more intriguing than his God who had brought me to Lochfeld in the first place. His empty library? Well, I didn't question my good fortune when that happened, which was frequently. He was the only priest in the immediate Lochfeld district and often traveled the countryside, offering prayers and absolution.

"So that's where you've been," I replied. "I'd assumed you were somewhere close by."

"It was a long few weeks, trust me. But he asked me to accompany him, and it would have been foolhardy to say no. Doctors were needed, even old ones like me. And selfishly, I rather enjoyed throwing myself in the middle of medicine once more."

I sighed and brushed my fingers against Laurent's cheek, which was almost too hot to touch. *I do what I can to make sure the balance of his heart and works are tipped toward good,* Father Gerritt had once told me. He had a relationship with my husband that I didn't understand—and probably never would. But the fact he still tried meant there was some part of Laurent worth saving, and I wasn't going to be the one to pray he met his end now.

"Is it truly as serious as Willem suggested?" I asked.

Father Gerritt reached for the rag again.

"I certainly hope not," he said to the floor.

CHAPTER FOUR

LAURENT'S OFFICE WAS SILENT AND DIM, BUT A FEW candles took care of the latter problem. The lamps that normally lit the room would have been preferable, but I didn't want to broadcast my presence more than absolutely necessary, for now that Laurent had returned to Lochfeld, the royal guard had also returned in force. Captain Willem and his men were the last people I wanted to see. Was rummaging through the king's personal documents considered treason? Perhaps—but I'd fought that battle when I'd first arrived at Lochfeld and won it already.

I shouldn't be here, but Father Gerritt's explanation of Laurent's disappearance and subsequent illness simply made no sense. He had advisors he could have sent to Harnow in his stead. For that matter, Meirdre had an army at the king's disposal, though they were rarely seen away from the borders and coast. Still, I wasn't about to accuse a priest of lying to me, especially one who had a hand in me still being alive, so I'd slipped into Laurent's private office unseen. There had to be something in here that explained what he'd been doing in Harnow.

As brave as I considered myself for being here in the first place, I didn't sit behind his antique desk. Instead, I pulled up a chair on the opposite side. My side. The safe side. The side where I belonged. If I was found on his, it would be obvious I was searching through his things, and some part of my soul wanted nothing to do with the responsibility of his side.

All these documents . . .

His seal sat on top of a mess of papers. Captain Willem had likely replaced it first thing after they'd carried Laurent upstairs. I lifted it from the right-hand stack of books and letters and placed it cautiously on the sliver of mahogany left exposed through the mess, half expecting a lightning bolt to strike me down as I did. There was no sound though, not even the creaking floors that signaled the sentry's passage outside, so I flipped open the first book underneath and rotated it toward me.

A calendar, it appeared. I knew Laurent's handwriting, and the last date was a few days after I'd left him sitting in the forest atop Foxfire, hollering after me. There was nothing to suggest he'd been headed for Harnow then, and I hated myself for accusing Father Gerritt, however silently, of lying to me. With a sigh, I closed the calendar and unwrapped the book beneath it. A few weeks of dust coated it, and I sneezed when I blew it clean. There was more writing in this one, hurried and squashed together, and I squinted as I tried to make out the lettering.

I will never understand why this responsibility was put to me—an irresponsible and selfish man. I haven't worn the duty well, that much is clear from the lectures I still suffer from Father Gerritt and the way Riette looks at me whenever she stands before this very desk.

I slammed the book closed on my finger and threw a cautious glance over my shoulder. Why hadn't Laurent brought his journal to Harnow with him? Had he left in a hurry? Forgotten it? Knew he wouldn't have time to write in it? The very fact I couldn't answer that question proved how little I knew about him. Would the journal answer any of my questions? I couldn't decide, but I flipped it open once more.

I've done wrong by her—by almost everyone in Meirdre. I know that. It was too late to earn Riette's trust and love as soon as I made that fool decision to have her whipped, and imagining I'll have the adoration of everyone in Meirdre is a delusion I won't allow myself. But it's not too late to do right by the people in Harnow, even if they'd rather see me underground than riding into their village. I can't cure whatever has befallen them this time—especially, heaven forbid, another outbreak of the measles—but I can manage supplies, pray, hold hands, and dare I say . . . help morale? Whatever needs to be done, I'll do it.

Unbidden, I rolled my eyes at his lie. Laurent, thinking he could help morale in a town full of peasants and commoners? I couldn't believe that motivation, and I found it hard to believe he could convince even himself of the words. Was it possible he was so paranoid someone would read his journal that he wrote falsehoods like this, hoping to cast himself in a positive enough light? That didn't exactly sound like him either —he rarely seemed to care what the court thought of him.

I flipped backward, finding the date when I'd first come to Lochfeld.

No matter what I told Willem last night, I'd be fooling myself if I didn't admit in private that she is attractive. Perhaps once she doesn't carry herself like a child playing dress-up, she'll become an asset to Meirdre—and me.

My lip curled. Too far back. I didn't particularly care to read what he thought of my body or my awkwardness at wearing nice clothing—though it was a relief to read that we had the same thoughts of each other. I would become the wife and mother of his children that his position required, and he would provide for my parents. Before I could lose my nerve, I flipped to the day after our wedding.

I have to admit, it wasn't the wedding night I expected. The girl cringes whenever I so much as look at her, so any intimacy is out of the question. She blames me for ordering the whipping, of course, but in time she'll come to accept that her choices were her own, and the consequences, too. Though I doubt she'll make the same decisions again. Even a peasant girl can learn what—

"And here I thought you scarcely knew how to read."

I gasped at Willem's voice and twisted around in my chair, my cheeks blazing. He strode inside, slipped around my frozen body, and gazed down at the book with a certain amusement in his expression.

"Instead, I find you so intrigued by the king's journal that every horse in the stable could have trotted in here without rousing you," he went on, lifting his oil lamp and focusing on my reddened face. "You must be fond of that dungeon."

I straightened my back at his threat. "Perhaps he should secure his personal documents better."

Willem cackled in a disapproving manner. I'd meant what I said, and he of all people knew I was anything but the king's perfect wife. Hadn't he shackled me in the back of a wagon halfway across the kingdom not so long ago? Delivered me to said dungeon himself?

"Maybe he should," he replied. Then, after a moment, "Though I see no reason his wife shouldn't be looking through his documents to make sure everything that must be done while he's indisposed is finished. It's a major reason a man suffers a wife, after all."

"Flattering." I straightened the books, only because my hands needed something to do but shake. "Thank you. I promise my intentions are all noble."

"You're welcome. Just be quiet about it." He turned to go. "It would be hard to keep the servants from gossiping, and I know you don't want that."

"Captain, wait," I called out to him. I didn't know why the question had appeared in mind—probably because I *had* snuck in here without anyone seeing me—but it had, and I wasn't going to let the one man besides Laurent who might very well be able to answer it get away. "Why is Lochfeld so empty? Your men, a few servants, a priest. But courtiers? A militia? Entertainers? Advisors?"

His forehead wrinkled. "He didn't tell you?"

"I asked. Once. He didn't answer, made up some excuse, and I never asked again."

"I'm sure he didn't." Willem shuffled his feet, then sighed. "The truth is, he can't afford anything else."

"Can't afford it?" I asked. "I don't—"

I wanted to laugh, but he sounded too serious. How could the king of Meirdre not be able to afford an entire court? Lochfeld had been built for more people. It could support more than the few dozen who currently occupied it. The books I'd seen as a child implied that a castle was full of people, royal and not.

"Then I can assume your meddling hasn't yet made it to his ledger?"

I shook my head.

"I expect the answer to your question can be found there."

With that evasive response, he slipped back out the door. I heard the hushed sounds of conversation, my name, along with an unexpected admonition to not allow anyone else in. Willem hadn't done much to protect me outside of the very basics of knife lessons since I'd arrived at Lochfeld, even though his comment was meaningless—no one would enter Laurent's private office right now. I was the only fool brash enough to do so. Still, I appreciated his effort. I was suspicious of his motivation and sudden good will toward me, but then again, Willem had rarely been outwardly hostile except when Laurent had demanded it. Yes, he was probably safe.

One of my candles had flickered out while Willem and I spoke, so I lit another and turned back to the desk. The sheer amount of paperwork on it was overwhelming, but a ledger of the castle finances? Likely in the stack under his seal.

And it was, three books below the journal. I peered inside the front cover, afraid of how complicated the system might be. Rows and rows of numbers greeted me, some in Laurent's hand, some in another. Not Juliana's neat script, but a blocky hand that didn't look as practiced. An erstwhile steward? Those entries were from at least eight years ago, and as I flipped toward the back, the king's own handwriting became more and more frequent until, finally, as of three years ago, it became the only one.

The accounting form grew less complicated as well: a date, an expense, a monetary amount. There was no running total, but my frequent checks toward the front of the book confirmed Willem's claim—Laurent had certainly cut expenses in recent years.

Or had he?

I ran my finger down the ledger. There were

certainly *more* entries five years ago, but none of them were over 500 crowns. Oil, food staples, horse supplies. Firewood, novel vegetable seeds for the castle's test garden. Tithes from both local and farther-flung villages offset them. Incoming candles, yarn, fabric, coins. All made sense. None were suspicious.

But when I skipped forward right to before I'd arrived at Lochfeld . . .

Several entries caught my eyes, each for over 5000 crowns. I tapped my fingertip next to them and focused on the entries in the expense field. All the same word. Laurent had almost scrawled it, as if its very existence offended him.

Horace.

I drew my finger in spirals around the page, trying to think. Large sums, an expense I didn't recognize—it certainly wasn't horse feed, since that was listed just above—and a castle with financial problems.

None of it made any sense.

But then, nothing about Lochfeld made sense. It was home to a map which called to me and illuminated itself to let me know where dangers troubled Meirdre, after all. Odd payments in the royal ledger were nothing compared to the power I'd come into when I'd placed the queen's crown on my head that day. They were certainly nothing compared to the fact that Meirdre was

one heartbeat away from having no monarch at all—
closer than we'd been in years.

Still, who was *Horace*? And why was Laurent paying
him large sums of money?

There was one person who would know.

CHAPTER FIVE

WHEN I TIPTOED INTO LAURENT'S ROOM A FEW HOURS later, Father Gerritt was gone, and the sun was even lower in the sky outside the closed drapes that still blew in the breeze. The sentry closed the door behind me, and I sank into the chair I'd abandoned earlier. The velvet was too warm in the airlessness of the chamber, and I began to wilt as I stared at the motionless figure in the bed.

What was I supposed to do? Simply sit here and wait until he woke up? It was probably my duty, as were so many other things these days, but it wasn't remotely one I could be happy about resigning myself to. To sit in the darkness and wait for something that might never happen? Surely there were better things I could be doing.

But as my eyes adjusted to the darkness, my heart skipped a beat.

Laurent was sweating.

Heedless of the warmth and the stray hair clinging to my neck, I jumped to my feet and grabbed a few rags, then pulled the covers down, cringing at the rash covering his bare chest. *No time for squeamishness.* As I wiped the sweat away, Laurent shifted, then coughed. My gaze jerked upward, toward—I gasped—toward his open eyes, dark and piercing. The room went absolutely silent. Even the birds outside seemed afraid to sing.

"Riette?" Laurent blinked several times. My name was a coarse growl. "What are you doing here?"

I sank into a curtsy before resuming my place in the chair at his side. He'd never want me attending to him while awake. Would he? I knew I wasn't courageous enough to do it.

"You woke up, sire," I said quietly, clutching the rags. "I didn't think—I thought you'd still be unconscious or sleeping. And I only wanted to make sure—"

"You shouldn't—" He coughed again. "You shouldn't be here. Go away. Now."

I leaned forward. "It's all right. I've had it. And even if I hadn't, most everyone else here is too afraid to do what needs to be done. Someone needs to take care of you." My hand reached toward his forehead, then back into my lap. Yes, it was easier to minister to an unconscious husband than a wakeful king. "Let me get you some water."

Laurent grumbled a bit, but he didn't argue as I poured a glass. He didn't even say anything as I mixed in some ground pulsatilla that Father Gerritt had left next to the pitcher, though his expression was wary as he watched. As though I was desperate enough to poison him. If that had been the case, I'd have done it long ago. Probably after he'd fallen asleep on our wedding night.

I hated to admit I'd have never actually done it. Leaving Meirdre open to Thomas's plans for it would have been worse than leaving Laurent in charge. I knew that now, somewhere deep in my soul.

"How long—how long was I sleeping?" he asked. "It feels like ages."

"I don't know," I replied. His hand shook as he reached for the water, so I held the glass up to his mouth, praying he wouldn't take offense. "You'd have to ask Willem. It's only been a day since you returned to Lochfeld. A few days, perhaps? I would think not quite a week."

"Willem." He said it as if he could barely remember that the captain of his guard existed at all. "I remember him shaking me, and praying, and then having an entire conversation with himself about what would become of Meirdre if the worst happened. I think he thought I was dying, poor man."

I think you might have been.

"It seems he may have underestimated you, sire, and Meirdre is better for it."

It was a cautious, respectful, and perhaps untruthful reply, but I didn't know what else to say. Would Meirdre be better with someone else in charge? Maybe not. I had the immediate realization that if I truly believed that, I wouldn't have agreed to marry him. For who agreed to be a crownkeeper for a man they truly believed was the worst thing for their kingdom?

"How do you feel?" I went on. "I've been especially worried about that fever."

That wasn't true—I'd been much more worried about his lack of consciousness, but one thing I'd learned in Elternow was to never let a patient know how worried you truly were. Worry led to panic, and panic led to . . . all sorts of terrible things. Laurent needed rest now, both physical and mental.

The beginnings of a smile appeared on his face, then faded. I couldn't tell if he'd remembered he hated me, or if he truly felt too weak to complete the motion. To my surprised, I couldn't tell which option frightened me more.

"I think—" He raised a hand and stared at the back of it, then let it fall back to the damp sheets. "If it weren't for this rash, I'd have sworn I was trampled by my own horse. Twice. I can feel every muscle in my body, and I've never had such a fever, even when diphtheria swept through Lochfeld when I was a child."

"I can imagine. You have been rather ill, sire."

"Just imagine?" There was panic in his question. "I thought you said you had the measles."

I sat back and rubbed my eyes. Heavens, his concern was beginning to wear on me. Where had it been the night we'd married?

She blames me for ordering the whipping . . .

I forced the anger down. It wasn't the time or the place—and if his journal was at all honest, Laurent had finally come to understand how desperately he'd hurt me. And it hadn't even taken years for him to do so. It didn't make up for anything, and it didn't make me trust him, not in the least, but it quite possibly meant he wasn't deranged or evil. Could it be he was simply afraid enough to make cruel decisions? Was it the only way he could think of to keep his power, follow through with his immense responsibilities?

Well, justifying his decisions wasn't my problem as

long as I didn't follow him down that path. And that, I was confident I would never do.

"Yes, sire, I've had the measles," I said, adjusting my skirts. "I was four. And since then, I've cared for the sick in Elternow with no ill effects, if you're that concerned. But no, I don't remember any details but the headache and constant whining that I wanted to be allowed out of bed and back to climbing trees with—" My breath caught. "With my friends."

With Thomas, I'd almost said.

Thomas, who still languished in the dungeon below us, after conspiring against king and kingdom. He was becoming easier and easier to forget these days, and I hated myself for not remembering him more often. Traitor or not, deserving of his punishment or not, I couldn't forget how horrific my own experience down below was. But Thomas had also betrayed me, betrayed our friendship, the steadfastness we'd shared growing up. The promises we'd made, even if, in the end, I'd planned on keeping them, and he hadn't. Maybe that disloyalty—how poorly he'd treated me before we'd been captured—was the most painful part of it.

Worst, if Laurent ever freed him, he'd immediately make his way to Vassian, and that would certainly spell the end of Meirdre. I understood why Laurent could never let that happen, even though my skin crawled when I let myself focus on Thomas's present situation.

"Good." A sigh of relief. "Good. I wanted to be certain. You need—you need to stay safe. For Meirdre's sake."

I should have taken offense to that—as though I only mattered to him as a tool he could wield—but I couldn't conjure up the feeling, even though he appeared more in control of his senses by the minute. His eyes had drifted closed a few times though, and there wasn't much time to waste. Maybe if he slept, he wouldn't remember what I was about to do.

Because if he did . . .

I took a deep breath before I lost my nerve. "Horace sent a message asking about you, sire. Yes, before I learned how ill you were. He seemed concerned. Should I send a reply?"

Laurent stiffened, fully awake. His body was wracked with a series of deep coughs, then his eyes narrowed in on me, predatory and fierce. But there was something else, as well. Dread?

"That bastard can't know what happened to me—nor what's going on in Harnow. He'll take advantage of my weakness, will— Iraela cannot learn that I'm indisposed," he went on. "Is that understood? Not even my mother can know. She will . . ." He sighed, apparently exhausted.

The kingdom of Iraela?

I set the rag on the table, to keep myself from speaking up and asking questions I shouldn't be asking. Laurent's mother now lived in Iraela—surely, she'd want to know if her son was ill. I would want to know if my child was doing this poorly, and I wasn't even a mother yet.

But—a strange glimpse of the future passed through me at the possibility of a child, Laurent's or not—maybe that's why he'd wanted it kept silent. It was probably humiliating enough for him to accept my assistance. No man, especially no king, would want his mother worrying for him.

But *he?* Who was he?

"All right. Yes. Of course. And they won't," I said soothingly, despite my desire to jump out of the chair and figure out what he was talking about. "Would you like me to stay with you? Call for Father Gerritt?" He'd want to see the priest more than he wanted to see her, that much I knew. "Or allow you to rest?"

"Stay." His brows creased as he reached out for me. "Whatever you put in that water tasted good, my dear. I'm going to sleep some more now, but I'd like you to stay with me. Maybe you can make some more when I wake up again."

"It's simply a tonic." I couldn't help a smile as I leaned toward him. "You have low standards, sire."

"No." He grasped my hand and closed his eyes. "I have high ones."

I squeezed it back, reassured that he hadn't noticed my questioning. He was still delirious after all.

CHAPTER SIX

For the next week, Laurent conducted his business of ruling Meirdre from his bed, tormenting the servants —who'd expected a reprieve from their sovereign's demands—with his drive to recover and bring the rest of the castle along with him. From the admittedly late seed orders for Lochfeld's summer gardens to his sudden desire for an inexplicable buildup of a militia on the western border of Meirdre, nothing and no one was safe from his need to prove himself healthy and in charge once again. Once his rash began to fade, Juliana and I took turns sitting at his bedside, alternately scribbling notes, filling his water glass, and running off long-winded courtiers or servants who took too long in agreeing to their duties.

Every so often, after a particularly thorough advisor

left, he glanced my way, his eyes dancing as if with a private joke—only for solemnity to replace it when he realized it was me and not his sister sitting there. I tried not to take it personally, but there was something in that brief expression that even I couldn't ignore.

Happiness. Hope.

A future with a man who might take the chance of loving me.

But could I love him? I wasn't sure.

Ignoring the question for the time being, I watched across Laurent's bed as one of his advisors, Garin Sinclair, rambled on about how the winter hay in his region had been decimated by an unknown fungus. How long had he been speaking? I could scarcely keep track of the words any longer.

". . . won't have enough to sustain the livestock over the winter if the infestation continues. I've already made arrangements to import more from the fields near the Illrus, but if—"

The constant droning on was too much. Sinclair was capable enough, Willem had informed me, so if he'd made arrangements, the issue was taken care of. He was here to air his grievances, nothing more. If the king had been stronger, I might have let him. Besides, he'd hit on something I needed to discuss with Laurent in private— those moldy haystacks, just like the ones Thomas and I had seen when he'd kidnapped me from Lochfeld. The ones he'd sworn had been burnt by Laurent's soldiers.

"Lord Sinclair," I broke in, "I will have a list of villages with a surplus for you in two weeks. You can request from them as you wish. Will that be satisfactory?"

Laurent shifted against his silk pillows.

"Yes, Your Grace." Sinclair stood, looking chagrined, finally. "Sire, my apologies. You surely have more important issues to concern yourself with. Health to you," he added with a bow, then disappeared.

Laurent raised his eyebrows at me as the door closed. "I've never gotten rid of him in under two hours before, and here you have him in and out in less than fifteen minutes. Are you part witch?"

Laurent, joking? Or was he trying to find a way to get rid of me? I gave the requisite laugh and adjusted my skirts. "Juliana told him I had your ear and that he disagreed with me at his own peril." A fool threat, but Sinclair had believed her. "All I had to do was smile."

"Outwitted by my wife and sister." He fell quiet, and I used the opportunity to stretch and open another window. "Not that I don't enjoy every second of it. If this is the price I pay for being unwell, perhaps I'll have to risk my health a little more often."

I stood there for a moment, watching him, then took

my place back at his side. His comment, playful as it was, didn't make any sense. He didn't enjoy having me around, and I didn't appreciate the lie.

"Juliana is the crafty one," I replied. "As I said . . . I only had to smile."

"Not so." He reached for my hand, and like a dutiful wife with a convalescing husband, I let him have it. "I've heard who wins at chess," he said, stroking my palm with this thumb.

My heart chose that moment to revolt against me, and I opened my mouth, then shut it again, too much in need of air to speak.

"Only sometimes," I managed to gasp.

"Hm."

It was all he said. Not even a word, only a sound. But the dismissiveness of it—not of me, but of Juliana's chess skill and her very existence in this conversation—shattered me somehow. He'd just made it clear that I was the only one in his world this very moment, and the realization was overwhelming, unwelcome, and the only thing I wanted, all at the same time.

Holding my breath, I leaned forward enough that I could draw his hand toward me, and then lowered my lips to his knuckles. Not as I had the night of our betrothal ball, as his subject in front of a hundred people, but as his wife—someone so starved for affection she'd risk his wrath or, perhaps worse in my situation, indifference. His eyes never left mine, but as his free hand reached for my cheek, I closed mine in a mix of fear and anticipation. One finger stroked my jawline, and I shivered, just as the bed creaked and his touch disappeared.

"Juliana rides for Iraela tomorrow," he said brusquely, shifting against the pillows once more. "I need you to accompany her. My mother is there, as you know, and it's time for our regular visit. I would have liked to accompany Juliana, but"—he waved toward the spots remaining on his exposed skin—"I don't see the need to worry Mother with my appearance. She'd never leave me alone if she knew I'd been so close to death, and I can't have her fleeing to Meirdre. Heaven knows I'm not infectious anymore, but I don't need her husband accusing me of bringing a plague to his kingdom, either. Do you understand?"

"All right." My cheeks were flaming, but if he was going to pretend nothing had happened, so would I, even if the pretense was all but worthless with the way I was shaking. "But what about the map? Iraela is so far away, and if I leave it unwatched . . ."

Laurent chewed on the inside of his cheek as he considered my question, then reached for his glass of water. "You'll be gone a month. Maybe two. As you said, you are not a prisoner here."

"I see."

I didn't, though. It was a drastically different statement than he'd ever made to me before. Directly, at least. What was he planning?

He narrowed his eyes at me. "Remember, your position as a crownkeeper is not something to be bandied about at the Iraelan court. Which is why you need to go, in fact. If my wife is rumored to never leave the castle, people will question why. Rumors and myth will soon become fact, and squashing them as quickly as possible is critical to Meirdre's survival."

But the alleged myth of the crownkeeper *was* fact, and no one knew so more than I. And even I didn't understand what it meant. How was I to do my duty, to protect my country, when I didn't understand how it worked, what the sparkles meant, how to decipher its warnings? I might not want to be a prisoner to the ballroom, but neither did I want to fail, and failure was all I felt now. I didn't understand the magic, and I needed to. What if the warning for Harnow hadn't only been about the measles? What if it had also been telling me Laurent had been in danger?

Fear poured itself over my head and washed the remainder of my desire away.

"Should I be going at all, sire? There seems to be much at stake."

I ground my teeth together. Too late, I realized I'd questioned him twice in five seconds, and questioning Laurent wasn't something anyone at Lochfeld did if they wanted to stay in his good graces.

Laurent didn't so much as flinch, though. "Keep your mouth shut, even around my mother, and you'll be fine."

He wasn't listening. Keeping my mouth shut was fine with me, since I had never been comfortable with anyone knowing my secret. *Secrets*, really, since I had many. Keeping quiet around the former queen of Meirdre would be an easy task. I didn't share Laurent's optimistic change in mood about the map, but it was true it'd been quiet ever since Harnow. The actual truth was that it had only lit a handful of times in our short marriage, and never for anything that would be earth-shattering should I miss it. And Laurent was all but ordering me from Lochfeld, wasn't he?

Yes. He was. And he knew better than anyone what was at stake.

Which meant everything would be fine.

Juliana, it turned out, while pleasant company prowling the castle together, was not proper company in a carriage. Her tendency toward traveling sickness overcame her more than once, and even though she insisted she'd be better once she adjusted to the roughness, I'd already figured out why her personal stallion was hitched with the rest of the team.

"I swear to you, Riette, it's never been this bad before," she said, clutching at her husband's hand. "All right—yes. I don't like how bumpy this is, and I'd prefer to ride, but it's too long for that. Midnight is only here for when I can't stand it anymore and need some fresh air."

"You don't need to apologize to me."

In truth, I wasn't doing much better than she, though indulging in Laurent's opulent carriage took my mind off most everything uncomfortable. The silk upholstery underneath me was just as fine as the silk I wore, the floor polished wood. It brought back memories of the map, and I murmured a prayer that everything remained well in Meirdre.

"She does. Because she's lying, of course." Berend, the Duke of Athnard, spoke for the first time in over two hours, roused from his slumber by his wife's claims. "It's why she's such an excellent horsewoman—anything to avoid the carriage."

Juliana tossed her hair. "You're jealous."

"I am, at that."

He smiled back, no animosity in his response.

Not for the first time, I myself was jealous of their interactions. There were fewer expectations of them than of Laurent and me—though I was certain they'd be happier once the king had an heir or two—and the love between them was obvious. Not forced, not uncut with acerbity, just warm and comfortable and ardent.

"Juliana," I said, reminded of the other member of Laurent's family who was currently in a happy marriage, "tell me more about your mother."

"Oh, Mother." Juliana waved a hand in front of her face. "She might not have loved him, but she appeared devastated when Father died, didn't leave her rooms for almost six months. We all despaired she'd ever be joyful again, and then one day . . ." She frowned. "One day Laurent came riding back with a marriage proposal from Iraela."

"A left-handed marriage proposal, darling," her husband broke in, apparently forgetting I was practically the victim of the same type of marriage. It was clear what the duke thought of that slight—with regards to Laurent's mother, at least. I wouldn't ask if he felt the same about mine and Laurent's. I had learned, over the course of my months at Lochfeld, to not ask questions when I didn't want to hear the answers.

"Yes, well." Juliana's hands fluttered nervously again. "Children weren't an issue, and it seems to have made them happy. You know she never cared much for what court life could give her beyond that. So much that I pray that she precedes him in death and isn't forced back to Lochfeld. The change might kill her."

It was a sharp reminder that Laurent's mother must have been born a commoner, just like me. Did Juliana feel the same around me, despite her kindness?

"The king of Iraela is happy because your brother paid handsomely."

"A dowry is expected," she shot back at him. "Even of a widowed queen."

I raised my brows. Short words between Juliana and her husband? I would never have believed it if I wasn't seeing it with my own two eyes.

"He sold her. If you can't accept—"

"Berend!"

Berend shrugged, leaned against the window, and closed his eyes again. Juliana looked at me, pleading.

"It's not as bad as it sounds," she said. "She once said that Iraela reminds her of her hometown. The palace overlooks a valley from its place atop the cliffs, and she speaks quite frequently of how she enjoys the views.

And her husband is—" She faltered a bit. "He provides for her very well, and that's all I'll say about that. It's not for us to criticize Mother's situation—or even discuss it."

It didn't sound like the love Laurent had told me about the night of our betrothal ball, but how could he possibly know the entire story? He must have felt secure enough in his mother's future to allow and bless her departure from Meirdre, and that was that. It certainly wasn't any of my business.

"I'm sure he does," I replied, with false assurance. I might have doubted Laurent's motives, but I had no reason to doubt his mother's new husband was anything but sincere.

The duke scoffed at my response. Juliana gave him a baleful look and closed her own eyes, leaving me alone to imagine what Iraela would be like.

CHAPTER SEVEN

IRAELA'S FOREMOST CASTLE CLUNG TO A CLIFF ON THE
north side of the Cresquet River, and even if it hadn't
reminded Laurent's mother of home, I could see why
she'd found happiness here. Like I'd done when I'd
arrived at Lochfeld, I watched it approach in the
distance, though this time I had to stick my head out the
carriage window while Juliana eyed me with
disapproval.

"Their guards are staring at you, you know."

I didn't so much as swivel my neck. "Let them stare."

For as amazing as Lochfeld still was to me, the home
of Iraela's ruler was beyond anything I could have
imagined. I couldn't tell for sure yet, but it appeared to
have been built into the mountain, for large waterfalls
tumbled on each side of the moss-covered barbican.

Above the guardhouse and keep, the main part of the castle seemed to hang in the air, suspended by nothing but rock and seeming magic. How could Juliana not stare like I was?

And I did, for the entire last hour of our journey, while Juliana fretted over her gown and her husband slept—apparently, the inns we'd stayed at had been much too quiet for him to sleep well at night. Part of me wondered if he simply didn't want to argue with his wife. Whatever the reason, I didn't care. I only wanted to look at the scenery and worry about how I'd look out of place in a foreign court.

My wariness grew as we rolled through the great gate into the courtyard of the guardhouse. We were all relations to the king's wife—some of us more than others—so a group of soldiers greeted us, all polished in red uniforms and with steel swords. Meirdre had an army, but a small one, and they were rarely seen around Lochfeld. I imagined these men marching toward my home, burning farmland, raiding barns and food stores, torching haystacks—

Torching haystacks.

The hairs on the back of my neck prickled at once. Laurent had so distracted me with his touch the other day that I hadn't told him of my suspicions. That Thomas had blamed the failure of the haystacks outside

Haszen on Laurent's troops, even though I thought—like Lord Sinclair had implied—it looked more like mold.

Maybe it didn't matter. I gritted my teeth as Juliana gave me final instructions under her breath—*hold up your head up, don't smile at the soldiers, give Mother a brief curtsy and nothing more, and then wait for her to speak*—and stepped onto the stone courtyard, wobbling a bit as I did. One of the soldiers approached me, and I bit my tongue, determined to make Meirdre proud, no matter how little I cared about Laurent's feelings.

Right. That's why you're thinking about him.

"Your Grace." The man's dialect, so similar to Meirdre's, was clipped. "The queen is waiting for you."

The disapproving tone in his voice made my skin crawl, but perhaps the formality was a custom. No one could control or even predict road conditions, and we'd come from so far . . . surely, she wasn't angry at our arrival time.

Then again, Laurent was her son.

I nodded and followed the soldier through a doorway, Juliana's footsteps comfortingly on my heels. It was hard to focus on anything but the beauty around me. The waterfalls, it seemed, were so in harmony with the palace that they acted as walls in some places and as pools with sparkling fish and lilies in others. I wanted to reach out and touch the water, but Juliana's reaction to my etiquette violation stopped me. Finally, as I was deciding it was worth risking her anger, the soldier stopped me with a soft tap to my elbow.

He may have introduced me to the woman standing in the parlor we'd entered, but I'd been too distracted to notice. I was not, however, too distracted to notice Laurent's cheekbones and strong chin, though I barely dipped my own as I curtsied.

"You're late, Juliana." Her mother—Elsanne—gave me the briefest of acknowledgements, then swept by me to plant the same brief kiss on each of her daughter's cheeks. "See that it doesn't happen again."

Juliana gave me an apologetic look as we followed Elsanne to the seating area by the window. Water roared somewhere in the distance. I adjusted my skirts as I sat, acutely uncomfortable.

"It's many days by carriage, Mother. Through a desert. You know as well as I do that schedules are fluid while traveling through the Mencote wilderness."

The duke, who'd been silent the entire time—I took that as my cue as well—rolled his eyes sideways at me.

"I wouldn't know." Elsanne reached for a glass a wine. "It's been a long while since I've traversed the waste between Iraela and Meirdre. And I was still practically in mourning when I did."

"Yes"—Juliana's hands fluttered nervously in her lap —"and we all wish you could return for a visit, but—"

"Riette." Her mother's attention swept toward me. "Where is my son?"

"He is—" I straightened, wishing I'd worn the stiff stays that couldn't help but keep me upright. Juliana shot me a cautious look, and my wish that I'd thought about a good lie before now joined my wish of harder stays. "He is quite busy, madam."

"Too busy for his own mother?" Elsanne narrowed her eyes at me. "He'd have never been so blunt as all that."

Laurent, you absolute dog! You could have warned me about her!

"No, madam," I replied. "Of course not—he's not too busy for you. It's simply—springtime is such a busy season at Lochfeld, and he takes his duties very seriously. I'm certain he'll pay you a visit as soon as he can spare the time. And in the meantime, I have a letter from him."

"Hmm. A letter. How decent of His Majesty." Elsanne shrugged and took a sip of wine, peering at me from over her glass. "I heard from Juliana that he refused to crown you."

I let out a breath, not quite a sigh.

"Mother!" Juliana, to her credit, sounded shocked.

"The king's decisions are his own, and you certainly don't need to speak of them in front of her."

"Oh, Juliana. You're just upset I betrayed the contents of your letter. Did you expect me to not be curious? It's not the Meirdrean way." Her attention swept to me. "Where are you from, Riette?"

For a moment, I'd already forgotten that the widowed queen had been a commoner as well. Even, possibly, a neighbor of mine from the past. For, of course, the ancient tradition of marrying peasants masked the only chance a Meirdrean monarch had of marrying a crownkeeper—the secret Laurent was desperate to keep.

"Elternow," I said quietly, hoping she'd never been there. I had no desire to speak of the fields that turned gold in the fall, of the poverty that my parents had escaped simply because I'd married well, of the rebels who preferred the small town for its position toward the center of the kingdom. There were simply too many good and bad things to discuss when I was unprepared to do so.

"Hmm," she repeated, sounding disinterested. "I've never heard of it."

I found that strange, since Elternow wasn't so very far from Lochfeld—the first village, in fact, where Captain Willem and his guard had arrived looking for a wife for Laurent. But Elsanne didn't sound like she was hiding anything—she simply seemed like a woman who had one thing on her mind, and currently, that one thing was harping on her daughter's choice of gown and criticizing her son's decision not to accompany me. I couldn't relate to Juliana's mother troubles—my mama was kind and gentle and accepting of almost anything that came along in life—but neither was I much surprised.

And with that dismissive comment toward myself and my history, she left me alone. I half listened to her and Juliana, pretending to be attentive, but my real curiosity was in the fact Laurent's mother had never returned to Meirdre since her wedding.

I lay in bed that night, listening to water rumble somewhere outside. It'd been captivating when I'd first arrived, but now it was an irritation. I wanted my own room at Lochfeld, the moon outside my window, the pattering of Sara's footsteps outside the door, the certain knowledge that Mama and Papa were safe in Elternow. Irrationally annoyed, I crept to the window and squinted out. Was I facing east, toward Meirdre? I had no way of knowing, but a fierce yearning washed over me like the water outside rushed over the rocks below. Was this homesickness? I'd heard Thomas talk about that before—even though his love for Elternow and Meirdre had been a lie—but having never left Elternow before the royal guard had showed up that fateful night, I didn't think I'd ever quite understood the concept.

I did now. To my surprise, I even missed Laurent—and that cursed map. Nothing here was familiar, from the design on the wool underneath my feet to the chest of drawers that sat to the left of the window. I ran my fingers over the top, desperately wishing for comfort.

And that's when I saw it, scratched in the corner of the lacquer.

Horace.

Horace? I stood there for a moment, staring at the name, then knelt and began to rummage through the drawers that one of Elsanne's servants had already filled with my things. It was odd, I thought, as I sifted through my stays and chemises, to not be allowed to select my own clothing for the trip—Sara had done that—but perhaps it was for the best. She'd always chosen more appropriately than I.

It was unlikely I'd find anything inside the chest, but I kept searching through stocking and silk slippers, hoping the servants who'd brought the chest to this set of rooms in the first place hadn't removed all indications of its past owner. But there was nothing, even when I slid a fingernail under the paper lining each drawer, and I knelt back, my eyes closed. Some hunter I was.

A knock at the door startled me, and before I could climb to my feet—or even look like I belonged there on the floor in front of the chest—Julianna made her way inside and cast me a bemused look.

"I was—I was looking for a gown for tomorrow," I stammered, trying to stand with some semblance of grace, yet failing miserably.

Julianna laughed and strolled to a screen. "Hanging in the closet, of course. But Mother's servants will help you dress—there's no need to find something yourself."

"Of course." I must have flushed, but she was used to my court missteps and didn't say a word as she pretended to look through my dresses. "Julianna—do you know who Horace is?" I pointed at the top of the chest. "His name was etched right here. No one's mentioned a Horace to me since we've arrived, so it seemed odd."

To say the least.

"Horace?" Her delicate eyebrows drew together. "I should say they haven't mentioned him— Iraelan rulers take regnal names. Horace is . . ." She made a face. "That's King Marius's birth name."

My mouth opened; my knees went weak. Laurent was paying King Marius that much money? Why? I clutched at the chest of drawers for balance, unable to ask the question, but unable to think of any valid reason for the numerous payments to a monarch of another kingdom.

Julianna, being who she was, simply attributed my sudden feebleness to traveling fatigue and called a servant, who helped put me to bed.

CHAPTER EIGHT

I SCARCELY ATE THE NEXT MORNING, EVEN WITH JULIANA'S constant prompting. No, I spent all of breakfast trying to convince myself that there was nothing untoward about Laurent sending most of his money to Iraela. A dowry, it must be. I'd have had my own if Laurent hadn't sent his men to my house that night. Nothing large like my own husband was paying his current father-in-law—a few goats, maybe—but I would have had one.

Dowries were a one-time payment, though. Laurent was making two payments a month. Large ones.

Juliana elbowed me in the side once more, and I looked up at King Marius of Iraela—*Horace* before his coronation.

"We do miss Laurent," he said, probably for the second time. "And I wish he could have visited as well.

But he did send an acceptable replacement in his stead," he added, lifting his glass.

I gave him a short nod. "It has been an honor to visit Iraela on his behalf, sir."

And now I want to go home.

I swallowed the impolite thought, annoyed at how it'd rushed into my mind, forceful and distinct. We'd hadn't been in Iraela much more than a day, and heavens knew I wasn't desperate to get back to Laurent. But perhaps... perhaps I was desperate to get back to Meirdre?

But why? My dreams of leaving Elternow had never been detailed, consumed as I was with the simple activity of survival. Girls like I'd been before the royal guard had shown up that winter night weren't supposed to dream of visiting other kingdoms or meeting foreign kings or eating the roast stag in front of me. Those dreams existed somewhere in my consciousness though, and since I'd married Laurent, they'd only become stronger. I wasn't an explorer, not in the least, but visiting Iraela had become something I hadn't known I'd desired until I was here. Returning to Meirdre should be the last thing I wanted this second.

My hand began to shake, and before I could spill my glass, I set it back on the table and clenched my jaw. Fear, absolute fear, overcame my annoyance at King

Marius's continued words, and I knew exactly what had caused it.

The map.

It was calling me. It certainly wasn't homesickness or any desire to create a relationship with my husband. If anything, I'd enjoyed being away from Laurent like I was certain he was enjoying being away from me.

It was the map.

I'd felt the sensation before, now that I thought about it, but last time—when Laurent had condemned me to death and his guards had tried to drag me back to the dungeon—it had been frantic. Now it was simply . . . disappointed?

In any case, it wanted me back.

And that meant—

I wanted to cry, but folded my hands in my lap instead, even as my entire body grew icy.

That meant something was happening to my kingdom.

Marius droned on for what seemed like another two hours, and I held myself together the entire time, though Juliana grasped my hand under the table, a concerned expression on her face. I shook my head each time she tried to elicit a response from me, silent or otherwise. There was no polite way to leave breakfast with a king, even if he wasn't mine, and I was smart enough to not even bother to try. I couldn't tell Juliana the truth, anyway.

But by the time King Marius stood, smiled at us, and headed through a set of doors on the far side of the dining hall, followed by a half dozen servants, I was frantic.

Grabbing Juliana, I pulled her into a private alcove, where water rushed on the other side of the open window, and tried to catch my breath. A lie. I would have to lie to her, since she wasn't, to my knowledge, aware of my status as a crownkeeper.

"Juliana—" Thinking quickly, I came up with the only excuse I could. "The king has called me back to Lochfeld. Immediately. He sent a letter."

"Really?" Her forehead creased. "Laurent wouldn't do that. He knows better. We never cut short our visits to Iraela. It's so far."

She sounded certain. Too certain. Would she ever believe my lie? She knew Laurent much better than I did, after all.

"Well, he did."

"Did he say why?" Her cheeks grew pale. "He's not ill again, is he? Riette—he seemed to be improving, but if he's taken a turn for the worse—"

"He's not ill—the letter was written in his hand, and the words looked steadier than they have since he recovered." Lying grew easier the more I did it. "But he didn't say why he wanted me back . . . at least, not exactly." Heavens, but she was nosy. "The letter was vague. You know how it is with him. I can scarcely contain my curiosity myself."

Juliana sighed. "I supposed it would have to be, in case the courier became curious as well. Strange, though, I hadn't heard of a Meirdrean courier arriving. They usually arrive near the beginning of the week. Well, if Laurent thinks it's important enough that you return home, I suppose you'll have to. If he receives a message declining his order . . . he might ride for Iraela himself, and we can't have that."

I could have kissed her for falling for my deception. "I'll pack immediately and send a new team for you as soon as I arrive home. It won't delay your return much, and if it does, I suppose your mother would be happy to spend a little more time with you. Agreed?"

She nodded, her eyes wide, like she couldn't believe I'd talked her into it—or that I'd rolled right over her desires in my haste to reply to Laurent's falsified summons. And when I waved goodbye from the carriage not two hours later, my trunk packed and attached, she stood in the courtyard with a half-smile, but she didn't wave goodbye in return.

When I arrived at Lochfeld days later, sore and dusty, the castle was even quieter than usual. A few sentries glanced my way and nodded as I padded across the courtyard and then up the stairs to my room, but no one else bothered me until Sara came knocking on my door an hour later. Wordlessly, she helped me out of my dirty gown and into a clean one, then did what she could with my hair. All I wanted was a bath and nap and to check the map, but I knew her ministrations meant something else was on the horizon.

"He's waiting," she said, jabbing another pin toward my scalp. "In the throne room."

"The throne room?" I spun toward her, momentarily wordless.

She nodded.

"But why?" Laurent knew better than to push things so soon after his illness, didn't he? "He's still not well. He should be in bed."

"Yes, well—good luck telling His Majesty that. He'll be back in his bed shortly, I'd imagine, but he informed me that he wanted to see you in the throne room, as soon as possible." Her expression said everything there was to say about my lack of choice in the matter.

Oh, no . . .

"Me specifically?" I pressed my lips closed. "He knows I'm home?"

Sara swiveled me toward the mirror for my approval and nodded. "And I would say that he's most displeased with you. Just a warning, my lady, since I'd never let you walk in there unawares."

My heart sank. I'd come back because something had happened to Meirdre, and Laurent was going to chastise me over it? I supposed that was his right, but that simple fact didn't make my immediate future any easier to accept. I nodded in return and slunk down the corridor, down the stairs, and to the throne room, praying no one else would witness my humiliation.

To my horror, Willem was already there, standing in the center of the room, his arms clasped formally behind his back. He turned when I entered, gave me a short bow—in here, at least, I did have some semblance of power, even if it hadn't been earned on my own—then walked out, his boots tapping on the stone floor.

Laurent raised his chin, and I curtsied, then peeked at him from under my eyelashes as I often did. He didn't look displeased, not exactly, so perhaps his quarrel had been with Willem?

Silly. He's furious with you about something.

"You're back at Lochfeld early, if I'm not mistaken," he began.

"Yes sire, but—"

"You will listen. Not argue."

Oh. Oh, yes. Sara had been right about him being angry.

I didn't apologize for my interruption, but my compliant silence must have been enough, for he continued.

"I thought I made it clear that you were to accompany Juliana. I didn't think I needed to specify that I meant for her entire visit. You have no idea what you've done—the problems you caused. From now on, you will do as I say, no matter how difficult you might find it. Nothing more, nothing less. Is that clear?"

I nodded and began to breathe easy once more. That was it? That was the lecture Sara had felt the need to warn me about? As reprimands went, I'd had much worse from Papa as a child. For that matter, I'd been subjected to Laurent's actual anger during our betrothal, and compared to being thrown in the dungeon and sentenced to hang, this was . . . nothing.

Or was it? Laurent didn't let things go so easily.

"Good. This may still be salvageable. Go back to your room and play with fabric or whatever it is you do. I don't want to see you for at least the next week—make sure it doesn't happen."

My vision clouded as rage descended upon me. He didn't need to warn me about running across him anytime soon; the feeling was certainly mutual. Cheeks hot with fury at his detached dismissal, I turned toward the doors at the opposite end of the throne room, then stopped and twisted back toward him. Laurent had already turned away and picked up a book, apparently secure in the knowledge that I would follow his latest royal command without argument.

"I'll leave you alone after you answer one question for me, sire. Why are you paying King Marius of Iraela 5000 crowns twice a month?"

He froze at my question, then stood and headed slowly toward me, his head cocked at an unnatural angle.

I didn't flinch. Perhaps it was his occasional kindness, but I was starting to realize that his threats towards me—most of them, anyway—were empty.

"How do you know about that?" he asked in an odd tone, too high-pitched for him. "Who told you?

I ground my slippers into the floor. "It was my responsibility to take care of the finances while you were ill."

Since you don't have a steward to handle the responsibility . . . and why not, Laurent? Couldn't you afford him any longer?

"I never asked you to do that."

To my surprise, he didn't blink much at the idea I'd

been in his study. Perhaps he'd already assumed I'd been doing some of the financial work while he'd been indisposed. If I was lucky, he wouldn't also consider the fact I might have been reading his journal while I was at it. For an instant, I felt the sting of the whip on my back.

Still, I scoffed, too furious to be afraid. "You were unconscious, sire. You weren't doing much of anything. I did what needed to be done for Lochfeld. So yes, I saw the ledger." My hands began to shake. "I saw all the payments you've made to *Horace*. While I visited Iraela and your mother, I put things together. If you meant to keep it a secret, sire, you shouldn't have ordered me there in the first place. And you shouldn't have assumed I was too stupid to figure out who Horace is."

"It was a dowry," he said through gritted teeth. "Even someone like you should understand that."

"Twice a month?" I ground my slippers in the floor. "Dowries are not recurring in Meirdre. Or Iraela—I asked Juliana."

In a flash, he was only a pace away from me. I supposed he meant it to be threatening, but my heart was not racing from fear. No, it was from the ever-so-masculine stubble along his chin and the memory of the way he'd touched my own that afternoon in his rooms.

Heavens. I truly was a fool.

"It is none of your business," he growled. "Stay out of it."

No. I wouldn't. I couldn't.

"I want to help," I said quietly, my shoulders sagging. "I can help. With—whatever trouble you're in. Please let me help you . . . Laurent."

The throne room was so silent I could hear him breathing as he stared at me. I didn't move, but his eyes flickered back and forth between me and a side door.

"Come upstairs," he said suddenly, gripping me by the elbow.

I protested until he reached the doors at the opposite end of the throne room, then stopped. Was Laurent swooping me off to bed?

No. He was . . . I had no idea what he was doing, truth be told. I flushed as we dashed through the corridors, knowing the servants would assume otherwise. By the time he pushed me inside his sitting room and shut the door behind us, my cheeks were on fire.

"Willem listens in the throne room." He gave my cheeks the briefest look before settling onto the divan by the window and patting beside him. "To everything. It's for my own safety, and I tolerate it as I must, but some things must remain a secret, even from him."

He was acting odd. Too odd. Heavens, the entire

situation was odd. Yet I sat, careful to stay far enough away from him, clutching at my gown to keep from touching my face.

"You can't help me." He looked at me as he spoke, but he wasn't seeing me. No, his gaze was distant, off somewhere I couldn't see and wasn't invited. "Please don't offer again. I can't have you involved in this. I won't allow you to become involved."

In what? was the obvious question, but something told me to remain silent.

Laurent glanced out the window and scratched at the back of his neck, then shook his head as if he were arguing internally with himself. Finally, he turned to me and spoke under his breath.

"She's a hostage."

"Who? Who's a hostage?"

His palm closed over my mouth, and my eyes widened in shock before I realized he hadn't hurt me. Nor had he been trying to, came the next abrupt realization. For the look in *his* eyes was nothing but panic and fear and a desperate need for someone to trust.

"Shh." He put a finger over his lips before releasing me. "No one knows except Horace—*Marius*—and me. And now you. Not even my mother is aware of her actual circumstances."

"Your mother? A hostage? Sire, I don't even—"

"She didn't seem like one, did she?" He shot me a wry grin, which faded almost immediately. "That's typical of her. But make no mistake, I worry about her every single day. And if I don't make those payments . . ."

I reached for his hand without knowing why. I didn't love him, certainly didn't want to touch him, but it seemed he needed me, and I couldn't leave him alone right now.

He clung to it, and I chanced the question. "What happened? How did she end up in this situation?"

He frowned at my fingers but didn't let go. "A month after my father died, a courier arrived. I didn't think anything of it at the time. It was an overture toward a more stable peace than we had enjoyed with Iraela in the past, and alliances are never something to dismiss prematurely. So, he and I talked. Then she met *him*. She was happy to leave Lochfeld for Iraela, and I didn't argue much or ask too many questions—I knew she hadn't loved my father, though she mourned his death as the end of an era, and I wanted to see her happy. I thought a change of scenery and someone else to focus on *would* make her happy."

He disentangled his hand and pressed his knuckles into his forehead. "And then the next letter came, demanding money. Not that he needed it, but . . . anyway, I thought it would be a one-time payment, but the demands kept coming. Don't pay, and not only does she die, but his troops arrive on the Meirdrean border that night."

I let out a deep breath. "I'm so sorry."

"Sorry. It's hardly your fault, Riette, dear." Laurent chuckled, a bit darkly. "So you see, you can't help. And you've no doubt angered him by leaving and violating my agreement—I was to send Juliana for regular visits as though nothing was wrong. It keeps suspicion off him. It was a poor agreement, yes, and I wish every day I hadn't made it. But I was rash and inexperienced and determined, and it was what I thought was best for Meirdre and Mother at the time."

Against my will, my heart broke for him. "And that's why you went searching for a wife as you did, wasn't it?"

"It took a few years to realize there was a solution staring me right in the face, but yes." Laurent nodded. "It was insurance against my fool mistake—though I never truly believed I'd be so lucky as to find a crownkeeper. But it doesn't matter. If Marius attempts anything now . . . I'm not sure we're ready."

My heart skipped a beat. He hadn't wanted to hear my excuse for leaving Iraela before, but now . . .

"Sire, I felt something while I was there. At first, I thought it was homesickness, since I'd never left

Meirdre before, but—but now I think it was something else."

"What?"

"I—the map, sire. Sometimes it calls to me." I bit my lip. Speaking of this in front of Laurent was painful. It brought back too many memories. "It did the day I saw Harnow for the first time."

He leaned away from me, toward the window, his brow furrowed. "The first time?"

Didn't he remember? Having to remind him was traumatic and humiliating.

I looked away, toward the desk which hadn't been there when I'd left. A candle burned on one side, and a familiar stack of books and documents under his seal lay on the other. Laurent was only playing at being recovered then, if he couldn't manage to make his way to the throne room except to reprimand me. Sympathy and anger warred inside me as I took another breath.

"I told you," I began. "I think I did, at least. So much of what happened back then is a vague haze in my mind. It happened when—when you took me to see the map. When I begged you to test me and see if I was truly a crownkeeper. When nothing appeared immediately, and I believed I was going to die, they began to pull me back toward—back toward the dungeon. And it called to me. I told you that much. And for an instant—"

I squeezed my eyes shut. I'd been so certain that had been the end for me.

"For an instant I thought I was simply afraid of dying, but it was the map. It wanted me to stay so I'd see something happening in Harnow."

Laurent cleared his throat, and his fingers touched mine once more.

"And when I looked out the window in my room in Iraela that night, I felt the same. It was calling for me, wondering where I was. And I felt—something like disappointment flowing from it. So that's why I told Juliana I had to leave."

When I opened my eyes, he was staring at me intently, his thumb resting on the back of my hand. "Do you think it will still speak to you?" he asked. "Give you another chance to see what you missed because of my mistake?"

I lifted my shoulders.

"I honestly don't know."

CHAPTER NINE

MY ENTIRE BODY ACHED FROM SITTING IN THAT CHAIR BY the ballroom window, but I hadn't moved from it in almost six hours. Sara had brought me tea and a light supper, and now as the spring air grew cool around me, I shifted in my seat again. Dancing hadn't appealed to me for some reason, but sitting no longer did. The map hadn't sparkled, hadn't glimmered, had just rested there on the ballroom floor looking to me like it looked to everyone else who crossed over its wood insets and borders.

Harnow had flashed white the first time I'd seen it, then white with red the second. I grabbed the journal I'd brought to the ballroom with me ever since I'd returned from Iraela. The colors had to mean something, *had* to, but unless the map spoke to me again, I'd never figure it out.

Unless it spoke to me again, I would never puzzle out its meaning. And if I could not puzzle out its meaning, how could I keep Meirdre safe?

And I hated myself for that. It might have been Laurent's decision to send me away to Iraela—and I supposed I could understand why—but he couldn't fathom the responsibility I felt as crownkeeper. I'd married him to fulfil my duty, all so I could live out my life at Lochfeld and protect Meirdre from the vexatious map that had probably sent the royal guard toward Mama and Papa's house in the first place.

But it wasn't speaking to me tonight. Realizing I'd fall asleep and end up spending the night here if I didn't stand eventually, I found my footing and crept out of the ballroom with one last glance back. In the darkness, with only the single oil lamp, I couldn't see the map, much less any detail. Shadows followed me as I strode to the library, and for the first time since I'd come to Lochfeld, the protection of Willem's men was welcome.

They dropped back as I entered, but the fire was still roaring on the opposite side of the expansive room, and the figure huddled in the chair across from it meant I wouldn't be alone while I searched. With any luck, he'd be able to help.

"Father?" I called, praying I hadn't disturbed a late evening nap.

Father Gerritt shifted around in his chair and waved for me to join him, the dark circles under his eyes more prominent than usual. "You've finally dragged yourself away from the map, I see."

"I shouldn't have, I don't think." I sank into the chair beside him and put my head in my hands. "I missed something while I was in Iraela."

"And that bothers you."

"Of course," I said indignantly. Sometimes his seeming mind-reading was too much.

"You know that's not your fault," he replied. "If he ordered you to go there and leave the map unwatched, he has no one to blame but himself."

I choked out a laugh. Father Gerritt was the only one in Lochfeld to speak that way about Laurent.

"That's not going to matter if whatever I missed harms Meirdre—or it affects me."

"Too true." He swirled a tumbler full of wine, deep red and syrupy. "Then we need to figure out what you missed and how we can keep it from happening again."

"I never leave Lochfeld, obviously."

Tears welled up before I could stop them. The very idea made me want to throw myself on my bed and sob like a child. I was petulant enough to know that was exactly how I would react if Laurent restricted me to the castle. Instead, I swallowed the peevishness and tried to let the elegance of the place wash over me. What kind of girl complained about being trapped in a castle?

"Nonsense. Queen Silke is known to have traveled the kingdom, after all. This isn't as much as a prison as you might think—you only need to figure out how she managed it."

"Silke." It didn't sound familiar. How many generations back had she lived? Father Gerritt had once mentioned the last crownkeeper had appeared over a hundred and fifty years ago, and it hadn't occurred to me until now that he shouldn't have known that closely guarded secret. "She was another crownkeeper?"

"Yes." He laughed and waved his hand at the shelves of books. "You learn quite a bit when you spend most of your time in the solitude of a chapel and library."

"Father Gerritt!" I jumped to my feet. "You never told me there were books about crownkeepers!"

"Ah, well, you never asked." He stood and ambled toward a locked glass case on our left. "And they aren't books, if we're being technical—they're the late Queen Silke's journals."

"Father!" My gasp was so loud as to be embarrassing. "And you never told me about them?"

"Yes, yes," he replied with a chuckle and glance over

his shoulder. "I should have said something before now. But you've had enough of an adjustment to royal life, and you seemed to be doing quite well on the map front on your own. Sara's spoken to me of the chart you keep. Have you noticed a pattern yet?"

I narrowed my eyes. Of course she had.

"No," I replied, shaking my head, "and I'm not sure I ever will, so let's go back to someone who might know. Have you read these journals of Queen Silke?"

He hesitated for a moment, then drew out a stack of handstitched papers tied with string. "No. They felt too intimate for someone like me to pry into—but you might have use of them, I think. Just don't tell the king. He'll wonder what has gotten into me, lending you such precious—and private—documents."

"Believe me, I won't." *Especially since I've read his as well.*

Father Gerritt handed them over, and I clutched them against my chest, stifling a sneeze at the dust that wafted up into my face. The writing on the first sheet was neat, with a date so long ago I could barely comprehend it. Only social niceties prevented me from running upstairs and reading page after page.

Or maybe to the ballroom, sitting right in the middle of the map.

"So, there you are." He locked the cabinet once more.

"You'll have enough reading to do for weeks on end now, which should make your self-imposed restriction to Lochfeld more palatable." He turned toward me and folded his arms across his chest. "But I suspect something besides missing the map's possible announcement is bothering you so much."

"Oh"—still clinging to the journals, I waved a hand in his direction, then fluttered it about my hairline in what I hoped was not obvious nervousness—"it's nothing."

Nothing I can talk about, anyway.

"Hm." He reached for his glass, took a sip, then set the drink down. "You found out about the payments, didn't you?"

"The—" Resigned to being surprised by his knowledge once more, I shook my head and settled back into my chair. "He said no one else knew."

Father Gerritt chuckled. "He says a lot of things. Some of which aren't entirely accurate—though this was close to the truth, mind you—just Captain Willem and I know the exact terms of the deal. Not even Juliana knows—she's under the impression her mother fairly ran off to Iraela to a new life. Laurent was too afraid she or that useless husband of hers would say something to the wrong person if she knew."

I raised my brows.

"Don't tell me you haven't thought the same thing about him."

Against my better judgment, I laughed out loud. "Perhaps. But, Father, it's a terrible situation. For Laurent's mother, for Meirdre, and for . . . for Laurent. Can nothing be done?"

"Without a war? Unlikely. Marius has a larger army, and more important, he has the desire for more territory. Laurent—Laurent doesn't want what territory he has now."

"But Laurent will protect us, won't he?" I stammered.

"To be sure. He loves Meirdre. But expanding? That's never been his wish. He never wanted a kingdom in the first place."

That was something, at least. I traced my finger along the edge of the table between us.

"But his mother is in danger," I replied. "I don't know how he can live with that."

"So are you, now. So is he." He lifted his hands in an indifferent motion. "He's lived with danger his entire life—it doesn't faze him. Hasn't since he was a child, I would imagine. Pragmatism suits him better, anyway."

I shifted forward and propped my elbows on top of the new reading material in my lap, an unladylike position I'd never consider doing in front of anyone else at Lochfeld. "He *sacrificed* her."

"I doubt she'd mind, even if she knew. She did the same as you, after all—married a man she didn't love."

"But she didn't know the story. She didn't go into her marriage and new position eyes wide open like I did. She didn't get to make that choice." I fell silent. Father Gerritt knew how difficult that decision had been for me. He'd been there in the dungeon, had walked with me to my almost-death. "That time around or this one."

"Not to sound unsympathetic," he replied gently, "but it's a little late to be worried about what may as well be ancient history. And don't forget what happens if Laurent doesn't fulfill his part of the bargain."

"I don't see any reason she'd make the same decision I did." I chewed on my lip. "But she needs to *know*."

With an odd look, he polished off his glass and stood to rummage through a drawer. "It is not my place to talk you out of this, Your Grace." He pulled out a quill and a blank sheet of paper, then said with a sparkle in his eye, "And you know, it's been a long time since I've participated in any rabble-rousing. Just don't"—he winked as he handed the supplies over and I added them to my stack—"tell Queen Elsanne I was involved."

Silke's journals were smudged, faded, and written in a style I could scarcely read. Even so, I lit one more candle as I hunched over the first book, my eyes dry and painful. There hadn't been much about the map yet, but her life had become real in the past hour. More than that, her very existence, the one of a merchant's daughter turned queen long before I'd been born, validated my own. Silke had been less thrilled than I had been with leaving her family and her own betrothed, but still, she'd come to Lochfeld for reasons I hadn't quite discovered.

The castle is cold and dark, with a certain lack of charm.

I had to laugh. Lochfeld hadn't been exactly warm over the past season, but somehow, I suspected Silke hadn't spent her first days here in the icy dungeon like I had. And lack of charm? I glanced at the tapestry that still hung on my wall even though the fireplaces kept the room warm in winter. There was charm here, from the oil lamps that smoked in some of the more closed-off corridors, to the false stained-glass windows in the library, to the stables where one of my few friends— however equine—lived. No, unless Lochfeld had been drastically renovated over the years, Silke was wrong about the lack of charm.

And this dreaded map. All the secrets surrounding it. The king believes it's some sort of magic, and perhaps it's that, but it's not as esoteric as he supposes. Can you believe the man asked me what happens when another village is built? As though if a new settlement wasn't installed on the original map, the magic doesn't work. Trust him to not realize any part of the floor can glow, not only those parts with existing villages—though I sometimes wonder if his dullness is a benefit to Meirdre. A dim-witted king can easily be controlled by others, and he is, thank the heavens, surrounded by competent advisors.

All that said, he's not the worst man to spend my nights with.

I slammed the book shut, blushing. *That* was too personal, especially when Laurent and I had never spent a night together. Not like that.

Maybe this was a terrible idea. I hadn't learned anything I wanted to know about Laurent by snooping through his writings, after all. Only that he still tried to justify his decisions regarding my treatment, still didn't understand why I could never trust him as my king or my husband.

Yet I couldn't help but wonder if things could ever be different. Juliana and Skylark made good company, yes, but they didn't take the place of a husband. Someone to console me when I cried of loneliness at night— someone who needed me to console him when things went wrong. Like I'd done, even if he hadn't known it, when they'd brought him back to Lochfeld, feverish and near death. Would he have let me sit by his bedside had he been aware?

And there were more practical issues at hand. Laurent would need heirs someday—sooner rather than later, I supposed—but there was no talk in the castle yet, and Laurent himself hadn't said a word. Perhaps he depended on Juliana to eventually fulfil that expectation with her husband, but how long could that last until the gossip began?

Beautiful as you are, I won't take what you're not willing to give without reservation. When you feel differently, you may ask for an audience and inform me, he'd said the night of our wedding. I hadn't felt differently since then—at least, not differently enough to acquiesce to his presumptuous demand and tell him.

With a sigh, I set Silke's journals aside and picked up the pen and paper Father Gerritt had given me. There was no use dwelling on Laurent when I needed to save his mother.

CHAPTER TEN

The letter that I'd handed off to the courier headed for Iraela was at the forefront of my mind as Skylark and I trotted along the forest path next to Laurent astride Foxfire. Most of me was unwilling to be on the trail so early in the day, yes, but Laurent hadn't exactly given me a choice when he'd knocked on my door that morning.

The servants are becoming suspicious of our lack of relationship, he'd said. *We need to be seen going off somewhere together.*

Dutiful as always, I'd called for Sara, who'd been nearly beside herself with joy that I was accompanying the king out of the castle, *alone.* I was less thrilled at the stays and gown she'd selected, both too elaborate for a morning of riding. Did she suspect something was wrong between us, as Laurent believed, or was she simply dressing her mistress as her station required?

Shaking off the question, I glanced sideways. Laurent was staring forward at the hanging vines like I didn't exist, so I stared at him in return, trying to figure out what kind of man could exchange his own mother's life for the safety of his kingdom. A cruel one? A desperate one? Desperate was probably better than cruel, but did it matter in the end? Did the ends justify the means?

Maybe they did. Maybe they didn't.

At that very moment, the answer to the question people had asked for centuries became even more impossible to answer, because the way the light reflected off Laurent's face caught my attention. A sculpted chin —though not arrogant-looking, unless you knew him— a relaxed jawline, and hair that was interspersed with gray despite his youth. Though it hadn't left any lasting physical scars, his bout with measles had not been kind to him in some regards. Like on the night of our betrothal ball, I suddenly saw him as a man—not a king —and it was a swift and not unwelcome reminder that he was also my husband. A husband who knew all the terrible things he'd done.

"I should feel flattered"—I jumped at his voice—"that

my own wife is staring at me once more. I wonder if I should dare ask how many times you've done it, and I haven't caught you."

"Don't flatter yourself," I replied, gripping the reins so tightly my knuckles went white. "There was an owl over your shoulder, sitting in a tree. I'd never seen anything like it before."

Laurent's brows rose. "You've never seen anything like an owl sitting in a tree? I hadn't thought Elternow, with all its faults, could possibly be as constrained as all that, my dear."

Miscreant. I was about to snap at his less than flattering comment about my hometown, but—was that a grin on his face? I looked away, lest I react in kind. Skylark tossed her head, displeased with my less-than-graceful control.

"Elternow is certainly not Lochfeld," I replied, guiding her farther from Laurent. "I would have thought that was understood, sire."

And a morning ride was a horrible, horrible idea. I should have pretended to be asleep when he knocked. Or sick. Or perhaps even dead.

"Indeed. But you don't dread waking up here every morning very much, do you?"

At first, I thought he was accusing me of enjoying the

periphery of his wealth and power more than I should, but at the true concern in his question, I twisted back toward him with a frown.

"Of course I don't mind, especially now. Please don't take this the wrong way, but I hadn't realized how content I was here until I came back from Iraela. I think I needed that time away to see it."

"No offense taken. Sometimes we need to lose something—even temporarily—to realize how good it was." He cleared his throat and gestured forward with a slight tip of his chin. "Up ahead is the clearing I've been wanting to show you since that day you ran out on me."

I flushed deeper and urged Skylark into a trot, past Laurent and his prying eyes. It was one thing to have run out on him that day but quite another to have him bring it up. Of course, he probably wasn't used to his speech being curtailed. Anything he thought, he said—as long as it benefited him.

But how did *this* conversation benefit him? I cringed to think of the possibilities as the narrow trail opened into a clearing, golden and warm, with a small spring on the opposite side. It was clear why the trail stopped here; the horses would be unable to make their way past the boulders and rock wall behind where the water left the earth. It was crystal clear as it bubbled into a small creek, and I suddenly felt very thirsty.

"This was worth riding with me now, wasn't it?" Laurent came to a stop next to me and hopped off Foxfire in one swift movement.

I nodded, wondering if he planned to help me down, or if I could escape from the opposite side of Skylark before he touched me. I'd ridden sidesaddle today though, and he'd trapped me neatly. With more patience than I felt, I waited for him to present his hand and then slid to the rocky ground with his assistance, my left foot landing squarely on a primrose as I did.

"I suppose I'd have never come all this way by myself," I replied. "Not for a while, at least."

Not after you ordered me back to the castle last time I tried.

"I was wrong, you know." He plucked a fresh primrose from the ground and handed it to me. "To insist you either go back to Lochfeld that day or come here with me. And I am sorry about that. You won't be happy if I keep you inside."

What do you care if I'm happy?

I stuck my nose in the bloom in an instinctive reaction, though perhaps it was to avoid looking at him and apologizing as well. The words were on the tip of my tongue, but it was he who'd wronged me. I wouldn't apologize for something I hadn't done.

Laurent sighed at my silence and pulled another

flower from the earth, this one a pale violet that shone in the morning sun. He considered it for a moment, then took a step toward me as I ground my toes into the dirt. His closeness made me want to flee, but before I could argue my own intentions, he'd tucked the flower behind my ear.

A long shiver ran along my back as his fingers drifted from my ear down my jawline. This was—

Silly girl.

This simple touch was better than kissing Thomas had ever been.

"What do you want from me, Riette?" Laurent asked under his breath. "Anything. Just tell me."

I shook my head as his fingers settled under my chin, the meadow still spinning about me. I yearned for him, as most wives would for their husbands, but fury was somewhere in there, for I knew his pretense at courting me had been for one reason only, but something kept me rooted in place, like the trees around us moved for nothing. But above my anger, floating and distant, was something I didn't want to accept.

"Nothing," I managed to whisper, though it was a lie. I wanted his companionship, his love, his respect, even though he'd sealed that fate months ago. "I don't want anything from you."

"I don't believe you. Everyone wants something from the people in their lives."

My breath caught. "Then you tell me first, sire. What do you want from me?"

Laurent was silent for a moment, then pulled away and ambled through the grass toward the spring. His disappearance left me cold, though the sun was warm on my skin, and for a second, I could only stand there and watch his back as he retreated. Grass swished about my ankles as I darted toward him, though I stopped myself short of catching him by the arm. He turned as I approached and, pointing at the water, smiled at me like our conversation hadn't ever happened.

"I used to play here as a boy. I would imagine the spring was the ocean, and dragons of old had returned, and I fought them, only for them to trap me at the edge of the world—just me and a sword."

I inched up to the edge next to him, wavering on the uneven rocks that surrounded the small pool. Laurent hesitated, then reached out. I wiped my palm on my gown, more to delay the inevitable than to dry my hands, then took his hand in mine. *Practical.* It was a practical move and nothing more. If I tripped, he'd have to carry me back to Skylark, and I'd die before that happened.

"And then what?" I asked. I didn't care much, but I had to distract myself from his touch, because the thoughts running through my head were definitely *not* practical ones. "After the dragons trapped you here."

"Sometimes I slew them. But most of the time—" He looked up toward the high trees above us, as if I weren't right there next to him. "Most of the time they slaughtered me, then laid waste to Meirdre."

I held my breath.

"You ask me what I want?" Laurent turned to me. "That's what I don't want. A childish nightmare that I can't shake, no matter how hard I try. What I do want comes second to that—always has. Always will."

"But if there were no . . . dragons? Ever?"

He scoffed. "There will always be dragons, whether they breathe fire or not. Meirdrean insurgents, foreign rulers bent on expanding their own kingdoms, pirates who steal the lives and catches of our fisherman."

I sank to the ground as gracefully as I could and tugged at a piece of grass. "You can have a life outside of your duty. Maybe not like others, but I think there's hope. Even happiness." Laurent stared down at me as if I'd just informed him that he'd grown another head, and I shrugged. "So? What do you want?"

He collapsed beside me and reclaimed my hand. "Something I can never have."

My heart skipped a beat. And that water next to us—when his fingers touched mine, I could have been drowning in it, for as well as I couldn't breathe.

"You have no way of knowing what's in your future," I replied. "Even I can only tell some things, and that's an enchantment most don't have. I think you presume too much, sire."

"Do I?" A laugh, but it was dark, especially in this breezy meadow. "I doubt that. But I'll tell you what I want, since you're so insistent. There's so much. I want you to call me Laurent. I want you to trust me, and to love me, and to hold my children during the day and me at night." He rubbed his forehead with the heel of his palm and sighed. "I want—" His voice cracked. "I want you to forgive me."

His honesty hit me like a rock, though it shouldn't have, with as hard as I'd been pressing him—a strength which seemed wrong now.

"Forgive you for what?" I asked, my voice breaking. "I want to hear you say it."

I expected him to hedge, but he merely took a deep breath. "For not valuing you immediately, crownkeeper or not. For not trusting you, for accusing you of lying—and worse, for sending you to the dungeon, for having you whipped, for treating you as though you were something unwanted."

I hadn't expected him to answer my question, and as the breeze tugged my hair from its plait, I couldn't do anything, couldn't even say anything. I could only grab the loose strands while I stared at him.

"Can you?" he added, as I sat there frozen. "Forgive me?"

"I think so," was my cautious reply, and to my surprise, I meant it. "In time."

Laurent's shoulders sagged in apparent relief. "In time is . . . more than I could have ever asked for. And I will do everything within my power to give you a reason to do so."

"Is that why you brought me here today?" I licked my lips. "To apologize?"

"Riette, dear. You're giving me too much credit on my planning ability." His eyes shone as he looked down at me. "I only wanted to ease the servants' suspicions—but this will do as well, as long as we can sit here a while without any other responsibilities."

Without another word, I shifted my weight to the side and leaned against him. A heartbeat passed—the longest heartbeat ever—then his arm wound around my back, drawing me even closer to him. We sat there for almost an hour, my head on his shoulder, listening to the water splash and the birds singing their melodies of spring. The meadow cooled as the sun traversed the sky, then disappeared behind a cluster of particularly tall trees, but it didn't matter. With Laurent next to me, I felt warm. Safe. Almost—almost loved.

And then we heard the shouts.

CHAPTER ELEVEN

I DIDN'T KNOW THE NAMES OF THE ROYAL GUARDSMEN who rode behind and next to us, but Captain Willem hadn't arrived with them—though no one told me what made our ride so urgent. My heart thumped as Skylark galloped down the path through the open meadow atop the cliffs. Anyone could see us riding back to the castle out here, but the guard wouldn't have ridden for Laurent and me in the first place if it wasn't safe, would they?

More men than usual prowled atop the walkways. Someone must have called them from the nearest village, and even though my soul screamed that their presence meant danger, we galloped on. In front of me, Laurent shouted back and forth with one of his guardsmen. We were safe enough, for now.

When I arrived in the back gate of Lochfeld, sore and windblown, I was pulled from Skylark before I could recognize the person doing the pulling or see where Laurent had disappeared. I yanked my arm away, prepared to shout at whoever was in my way, then stopped.

The man who'd pulled me from my horse wore the uniform of the Meirdrean army.

I backed against Skylark in shock and more than a little fear. Meirdrean soldiers patrolled the border for protection and deterrence, or, if the unthinkable happened, for war. They didn't appear anywhere else, even at Lochfeld.

Was this—was this war?

"You need to come inside, Your Grace," he said. My eyes darted from the sword at his side to the group of soldiers beside him. "It's not safe for you out here."

I tried to spit back some argument, but our dash from the springs had stolen both my breath and desire to squabble. Instead I nodded, and he followed me inside, my riding clothing a stark contrast to his deep blue jacket. Brushing the dirt and grass from my skirts didn't make me anymore presentable, so I lifted my chin and pretended I didn't care what any of them thought. That performance became more difficult when he escorted me to a small room in the old keep, and Sara sprang from a chair in the corner.

"Oh, there you are!" She circled around me, her hands fluttering until they finally landed on my disheveled hair. She swept away a few leaves, then stood back and examined me. "Are you all right? Did anything happen?"

"I'm fine." I swatted her hand away as the soldier nodded and shut us inside. "It was a pleasant ride until we were interrupted—not that I'm all too surprised about that, I suppose." To tell the truth, I was a bit irked about my day with Laurent being taken away. "But what's going on?"

Sara exhaled, then circled about the room, her eyes darting from me to the floor to the door. I watched her pace, my forehead drawn. Sara was frequently anxious, but not like this.

"They came a few hours after you left," she said, fussing with the pins in my hair. "Overcame the guard and headed for the dungeon."

The dungeon.

"They? Who's *they*?" An odd feeling welled up in my gut. Edgy, twitchy, a combination of wrath and dread. "They came for Thomas. Didn't they?"

"That's what they told me. The soldiers, I mean, and I think they're the only ones who know what's going on at this point. Willem sent for them before—" She pulled a pin from my hair and fell silent.

"Before what? Before what, Sara?"

Sara twisted the pins around between her fingers.

"Before they killed him."

I had no idea what was going on in the rest of the castle. Male voices echoed in the hallways, but none belonged to the servants I was used to hearing. My temporary shelter must have been hastily planned, for besides the chair Sara had relinquished to me, there was no furniture, and she'd grabbed no embroidery to pass the time. I alternately sat and paced, and, at one point, when the sun disappeared under the high window, stuck my head outside the door.

The soldiers standing guard simply told me to go back inside.

I agreed with no argument, but I was screaming internally. I needed to see the map. Didn't they understand that? Of course they didn't, but once more, I'd left the castle and missed something.

Or had I? Would the map have shown the attack on Lochfeld, the assault on the dungeon, Willem's murder?

Of course it would have. All those things affected the security of Meirdre, didn't they?

Yes.

In the worst way.

And it was my responsibility.

By the time a knock sounded on the door hours later, I was beyond caring that the floor hadn't seen a mop in fifty years. It was more comfortable than the chair, and Sara agreed, so we sat on the hard stone while she tried to make me somewhat presentable, for no other reason but to make time pass faster. I'd hoped, simply because she'd failed in that regard, that the knock wasn't Laurent, but when the door opened, he stood there, looking quite possibly more unkempt than myself.

I sprang to my feet and curtsied. "Sire—"

He gestured Sara out, and it looked like she couldn't escape fast enough. Did she know something I didn't? She regularly left to bring me my meals, after all.

The door closed, and Laurent spoke.

"You did this," he said. "You allowed them in."

"I *what?*" He'd sent me up to the keep for my own protection, yes, but the dungeon where I'd spent too many days suddenly seemed so close. So dark. So cold. "You think I—you think helped them break into Lochfeld and free Thomas?"

"It only makes sense." Laurent folded his arms and began to pace the chamber, stopping only to lean against the door. "You agreed so easily to our ride this morning. You flattered me. Stalled. Knew the guards would be with us, and not at Lochfeld. Told me things I wanted to hear and things you knew would keep me in that meadow until it was all over."

My mouth went dry. He couldn't honestly believe—

But it all made sense. Call it fate, call it bad timing, but he was right. My easy agreement made sense through his eyes. And I *had* enjoyed our ride, enough to stretch it out and spend time learning more about this man I'd agreed to marry. Had I'd known my vulnerability and forgiveness would have proven suspicious just hours later . . .

"Don't try to convince me otherwise. I can't believe a word you say anymore." He cracked open the door and slid outside to address the guard. "She's not to leave. At all."

My skin heated, becoming raw when I brushed my fingers together.

"But what about the map?" My panic should have been obvious—how could it not be? "You know I have to be allowed downstairs to see the map!"

"You missed it once." His expression was cold, dead —the exact opposite of that day in the clearing. "Maybe more than that, for all I know. Missing it again won't be the end of the world."

With that, he slammed the door shut, and his footsteps down the corridor were the only thing I could hear.

The chamber in the keep's upper floors wasn't as dirty and cold as the dungeon I was so familiar with, but neither was it the comfortable room I'd grown so used to. The soldiers had brought me a blanket, but I couldn't ask them to bring Silke's journals, and the very idea that Laurent could stumble upon them while searching my room for evidence of my *alleged* collusion with Thomas was disconcerting. It wasn't as though there was anything in them unfit for his eyes—*I hoped*—but my curiosity in them felt too intimate. He had no right, anymore, to know what interested me, even if it was nothing more than the scribblings of a long-dead queen.

The soldiers protecting Lochfeld thought they knew what interested me, though. Laurent, out of compassion or some sense of guilt—or perhaps more likely, vanity—had allowed Sara to bring me a few gowns, and the change in my appearance seemed to change the soldiers' behavior toward me . . . which on second thought, might have been why he'd permitted it.

A few days after Laurent had locked me away, one of them, a lieutenant almost as young as I, knocked on the door. I was certain he hadn't expected me to be dressed in silk.

"Your Grace, the king has commanded me to escort you to the ballroom and . . ." The lieutenant's brow creased. "To wait with you."

Well, at least Laurent had listened to me, though I was fraught with rage that he wanted me to watch the map even while once again accusing me of treason. And while lying about my ability and placing the continued secrecy on me, no less.

I shouldn't have been surprised. He was mourning the deaths of his personal guards and Willem, in particular, but with them gone, only a handful of people at Lochfeld knew of my power—if any. This young lieutenant—I gathered from his wording—did not.

"It was kind of him to allow me to stretch my legs," I replied, standing shakily. What I really wanted to say was *why* Laurent *actually* wanted me in the ballroom. But hadn't my mouth gotten me into trouble before? I could always tell him later, but I couldn't take it back if I mentioned it now. "May I know who's escorting me?"

The lieutenant gave me a cautious smile, and I almost laughed.

"Jonas," he said, the smile turning to a frown. "Jonas Vahl."

Perhaps realizing he'd been too familiar with the king's wife turned prisoner-or-whatever-I-was, he cleared his throat and gestured down the corridor. The keep had warmed over the past few days, and I breathed a sigh of relief as we entered the ballroom, cool as always. Those thick stone walls of Lochfeld had more than one use, I was discovering.

I ignored the chair next to the window—I'd done all too much sitting lately—and gave the map a cursory glance as I circled the ballroom. My pacing probably made Lieutenant Vahl uncomfortable, but I didn't care— I was more concerned with the map. I hadn't felt it calling to me while I'd been trapped upstairs, so it was unlikely it would speak to me today. Then again, maybe it sensed I was nearby and checking on it. Unlikely . . . but not impossible. I'd just have to wait and see.

Sensing everything in Meirdre was calm enough for the moment, I turned back to Lieutenant Vahl.

"Lieutenant, there are some journals in my room. On the desk underneath the window. Would it be possible—"

"The king said you weren't allowed anything from your room besides some clothes." He cleared his throat again and glanced out the window, clearly trying to end the conversation.

"Yes, but what if you were curious about what you might see in there? What if you suspected I truly was collaborating with Thomas Wennink, and that there might be information in those journals that would prove it?"

He shot me a sharp look. "Were you collaborating?"

"Maybe you should check and find out." I stood and meandered toward the center of the ballroom. Something was flickering there, but it was probably just the afternoon sun. At least, that was what I tried to convince myself as I rubbed my eyes and tried to ignore Vahl.

"I don't appreciate being forced to guard wily women, Your Grace," he added.

A choked laugh rose in my throat. Yes, I may have acted as a lookout for Thomas a few times, but *wily*? No one who'd known me for more than ten minutes would ever describe me as *wily*. Not even Laurent.

My amusement died almost immediately. If Vahl thought I was devious, he'd never take his eyes off me. But did it matter? What was I thinking? That I'd escape Lochfeld, and . . . and then what? My loyalty was to Meirdre and Laurent, even if he refused to believe me.

"I doubt you know anything about women." My argument was weak, but anything else would be a confession. "But I'm certain you know about following orders."

"I know that a loyal Meirdrean subject, fairer sex or not, shouldn't joke about treason. I also believe the king's wife shouldn't joke about anything."

He had no idea. I waved him off and focused on the glittering that coalesced on the floor. It was a royal blue this time, interspersed with gold flecks that shimmered every time I blinked. I rubbed my eyes and tried to focus while Vahl continued his reprimand. The shimmering curtain waved and stirred, moving from the Galvan Sea west toward—

"Riette?"

Rapid blue flashes turned to a deep green. My heart raced as the curtain became thicker and more opaque, narrowing in on . . . on Lochfeld?

No. It couldn't be.

But Thomas had escaped, hadn't he? The map warning me of danger to the castle wasn't beyond the realm of possibility. I ground my palms into my temples, praying the map would change, that the sign would move somewhere far away, out to the desert, perhaps, signaling a dust storm that wouldn't affect anyone. But the splendor of the magic hovered over Lochfeld, then settled into the mahogany castle inset in the floor.

I cried out, though it was a weak sound I doubted anyone could hear.

"Riette, what's wrong?"

"Nothing's wrong," I snapped. I wasn't much given to any kind of royal protocol, but Vahl using my given name was a line I wouldn't allow him to cross, if only because it would infuriate Laurent, and there was already enough trouble. Plus, his voice was adding to the headache that sometimes appeared when the map was revealing its power. "Please stop talking."

"I simply came to check on you." The voice shifted into a familiar tenor. "But if you'd rather I go away, I could do that."

Frowning, I tore my attention from the map, only to see Father Gerritt standing there. Vahl stood behind him, his arms crossed.

"No." I turned toward the glittering version of Lochfeld once more, then back to him. "I thought you were someone else."

"Let's talk, then. Somewhere else." He made to guide me away from Vahl, but the lieutenant closed in on both of us.

"Father, I'm sorry, but she's not to speak with anyone alone."

Father Gerritt gave him a single look and practically dragged me to a far window. I protested his ignorance of whatever rule Laurent had placed upon me, but he glanced backward once to Vahl—standing there with his hands on his hips right over where Lochfeld shimmered —and raised one eyebrow.

"If you give in that easily, you're not the person I thought you were," he said. "Unless it's true, as he said, that you were responsible for Thomas Wennink's escape."

"Oh, please." The rude reply tumbled out, before I realized that no one except Laurent and I knew what had transpired between us at the spring. "I had nothing to do with it. Why would I? I might not want Thomas dead, but I certainly want nothing to do with his plans or him personally. I'm Meirdrean, and I won't let him get away with what he wants to do to our kingdom. Besides, I think—"

I think I'm falling in love with my own husband.

The ballroom began to spin around me, but that time, it wasn't the power of the magic, although a quick glance over Father Gerritt's shoulder showed Lochfeld still shimmering, invisible to everyone in the castle but me. No, the spinning was my own emotions, both overwhelming and so welcome I could comprehend the combination.

Because I *couldn't* love Laurent.

It wasn't possible, and it wasn't the intelligent thing to do, and it wasn't like me. I wasn't given to forgiveness —at least, I didn't forget—and I certainly shouldn't choose to tie myself to a man who had the power and opportunity to hurt me. Laurent was an arrangement. A contract. He financially supported my parents, so I married him. For heirs, yes, but more importantly, so he'd have a chance of acquiring a crownkeeper as a wife. We'd both been lucky in that regard, but even after our conversation about dragons and forgiveness, that was all it was now—an agreement.

Or was it?

"You think what?" Father Gerritt asked.

I shook my head, my mouth gaping. This was too intimate for even him to hear. Once again, Laurent had betrayed me, and so my loyalty now should have been to Meirdre and Meirdre only. Only it wasn't.

"Nothing. I just—"

"Has the map spoken?"

"Right now," I said, pointing before I remembered he couldn't see it. My feelings about Laurent had to wait until I could process them alone. Even without Sara. "I need to talk to the king."

"About what?"

I swiveled at Vahl's question.

"About—" I looked at Father Gerritt, but he only shrugged his contempt of Vahl's curiosity. "That's not your business. But I must see him." Because *Lochfeld* was in danger this time. Laurent would want to know, no matter how furious he was at me, no matter how much he distrusted me. "You have to let me talk to him!"

Vahl blew out a deep breath. "He gave orders, Your Grace. He doesn't want to see you. Besides, it's time to go back upstairs. You were given an hour, and you've had almost that."

Laurent didn't want to see me? Even with news of the map? Then what was the point of letting me see it— or of keeping me alive? Father Gerritt looked like he didn't have the answers to those questions either, so I gave in and let Vahl escort me back to my prison— mostly so neither of them could see my tears.

CHAPTER TWELVE

Sara set the pen and paper down in front of me and frowned.

"If you don't feel like writing to your parents, I'm sure they'll understand," she said.

"It's been months since I sent a letter." I drew the paper toward me. Laurent had allowed me a small table for just this purpose—I suspect he was hoping I might feel guilty enough for a written confession—but it was an awkward height for writing. "And they'll begin to worry if they don't receive one soon."

She eyed me sideways as she hustled around the almost-empty room, pretending to tidy it. "Do you miss them, Your Grace?"

The pen skipped as I began the first stroke of the salutation, so I set it down and sighed. "Of course. But it's not as though I can visit." A sudden thought occurred to me, and I glanced her way. "Do you see yours often?"

"My mother"—her hands fluttered as she tried to smooth the wrinkles from my spare gown—"I haven't seen her in five years."

I scratched a brief greeting to Mama and Papa, then set down the pen. "But why not? If you need time—"

"Oh, it's not that." Sara pressed her lips together. "It's not important."

I blinked at her, then shut my mouth. In another world, I'd have pried the information out of her, but trusting Laurent's wife with an obvious secret? I couldn't ask that of her. It was an isolating realization, even as I gave the gold pen another glance.

"I'm sorry," I said, simply. "And I hope that changes soon."

"I'm sure it will." I could tell it was a lie. "But you— you could visit yours, if he allows."

A broken laugh burst forth. "He has me locked in the keep because he thinks I'm responsible for Thomas's escape. A visit to Elternow is hardly in his plans for me anytime soon."

She settled on the floor, against the wall, and adjusted her skirts. "If that was truly the case, you'd be in the dungeon."

I fought to hide a shudder. Sara didn't know I'd

already spent time there. But did she have a point? Laurent had already proven he had no qualms about accusing me of treason . . . though I supposed I'd confessed the first time around.

"Perhaps you're right." I managed to keep my voice steady. "But he doesn't seem to believe anything I say right now."

Sara made a noise of assent.

"Do you believe me?" I asked.

"Of course!" Her brow creased. "I've seen the way you look at him. Why would you risk that for a love affair with a rebel?"

"The way I look at him?"

Did I look at Laurent like that? My blazing cheeks didn't lie, but they did catch me off guard. I hadn't realized I'd begun looking at him with anything but disdain . . . nor that anyone had noticed the change.

"We've all noticed," Sara said in reply to my unstated realization. "And yes, he might not believe you now, but he will. He has to. Now finish that letter, Your Grace, and I'll have a rider send it out. You likely have time before he sends for you again."

Still, as the soldiers escorted me downstairs almost a week after the progress Laurent and I had made in our relationship had been shattered, I realized he couldn't avoid me forever. Whether I next saw him as his wife or semi-prisoner remained to be seen. Even more confusing were my allowed visits to the ballroom—if Laurent didn't want to hear from me, why was he bothering to allow me to view the map at all?

I asked myself the question over and over as we descended the stairs, but when we turned away from the ballroom and toward the rear courtyard, I protested. The soldiers weren't taking me to the dungeon, that much was clear, but neither were we headed for the ballroom and my daily check of the map. Perhaps Laurent's secrecy had backfired. The soldiers, especially Vahl, didn't know of the reason behind my visits there, and if they'd decided to change up the routine and take me outside out of some misguided sense of compassion . . .

Laurent would be furious, and I didn't want to deal with that, either.

"This isn't the way to the ballroom," I said.

"As though you ever dance while you're there, anyway. I'm starting to believe you don't know how." Vahl shrugged. "But you're right—we're not going to the ballroom today. You should be grateful for the longer walk."

He thought Laurent was allowing me to visit the ballroom so I could practice dancing? I could have laughed, but the sheer number of strangers passing us in Lochfeld's corridors, soldiers and mercenaries both, brought a sense of dread to my very soul. And Laurent's vague intentions for me today had already worn on my nerves. Was Vahl taking me to see him?

"I don't dance with others watching," I replied.

"Well, since you're going to be watched, I guess you don't need to be in there."

He motioned toward an iron door I'd never given much attention to. Probably just another cold storage vault. Not for the first time, I wished Juliana and I had explored more, but after my time in the dungeon, I preferred to stay in the more updated parts of the castle. Anything to keep from being reminded of Lochfeld's original purpose as a fortress, and the horrid things that had—and still happened—here.

"What is this?" I asked as Vahl pried open the door.

"The war room," he replied.

War room?

It took a moment for my eyes to adjust, even though a dozen oil lamps illuminated the octagonal room. If the keep was secure, this room, windowless and cool, was a fortress.

And there Laurent was, leaning over a large table in the center of the room. A map of the entire region covered it, though unlike the one in the ballroom, it was stone, and I assumed it wasn't magic. A dozen miniature men, painted dark blue like Vahl's uniform, were spread across Meirdre, tiny beacons of protection.

Laurent waved Vahl away, and I flinched as the heavy door clanged shut, trapping me with him. I didn't curtsy, and he didn't say anything about that—maybe because I'd shivered at the same time, from both the chill in the room and the heartbreaking expression on his face.

"They killed him," was how he greeted me instead. "Killed him and left his head in front of the throne. Like he was something to throw away, someone whose sole purpose was to send me a message."

My knees went weak. Laurent didn't sound angry, even at the ones who'd done this. Grieving, yes, he sounded like that. When he looked at me, his stare was distant, not furious as it'd been when I'd last seen him. He was dressed as suitably as ever, though an empty scabbard hung at his side—unusual for him—but the usual arrogant manner with which he wore silk had vanished since I'd last seen him. He was acting now—as a king, as someone who had everything together, as a man who still had control over his life. The reality was, he was devastated.

"Captain Willem?" I asked, though I didn't need to.

"And six of his men." Laurent nodded as he approached me. "Fifteen years of service, all taken in the blink of an eye, all because I was careless."

"Careless how, sire?" He stopped and considered the floor when I spoke, and I realized he had absolutely no idea how to answer that question—and that he'd somehow learned I had nothing to do with Thomas's escape. "Because you allowed yourself to be happy for five minutes?"

His chin jerked up. "They did not need to lose their lives because I was off courting a woman."

"Not a woman. Your wife." Laurent's eyes flared at my impertinence, and I went on, quickly. "And forgive me for saying so, sire, but you are not trained in war—at least, not like Captain Willem and the rest. If you were so trained, if you were so confident in your ability to take on the enemy alone, you wouldn't have soldiers here now. If you'd been inside the castle that day, who knows how things might have ended? You dead. Meirdre lost."

"I have fought. Maybe not in all-out war, but I'm hardly inexperienced." His forehead creased. His stance grew rigid as he waved back at the table and map. "Who do you think helped force the Nantoisens back across at the border at Vistel over the winter?"

"I know you did." It seemed different to me, though I knew it didn't seem so for him—maybe dragons really were dragons, even if some were more dangerous than others. "And I am sorry he's gone. I'm sorry Lochfeld feels less like a sanctuary for you than it did. And I'm sorry you blame yourself for what happened."

"But not you."

"I'm sorry, sire?"

"I don't blame you, and I was wrong to do so." Laurent sighed and glanced up at the ceiling. "We captured one of Wennink's rebels yesterday. He confessed to everything—that King Damir of Vassian had set things up, that he'd requested they raid Lochfeld and attempt to rescue Wennink. He was paid handsomely by Damir, from what I understand, though he didn't live long enough to enjoy that new wealth."

For a long time, I didn't know what to say. Thomas had made a deal with Damir at least a year ago: once Laurent was dead and Meirdre thrown into disarray, Vassian would use its armies to take over our kingdom. But Thomas's continued survival was key there. Damir wouldn't make a move until Thomas appeared in Vassian to assure him there would be no protracted war over Meirdre.

That plot was one of the biggest reasons I'd agreed to marry Laurent.

I didn't want to be the one to point out that Laurent would have gone on believing I was involved had they not been lucky enough to capture one of Thomas's men. The trust between us was already splintered, and the king of Meirdre had a more urgent problem, made evident by our current location and the army movements playing out on the map between us.

The Kingdom of Vassian wanted Meirdre.

And they were ready to make their move.

CHAPTER THIRTEEN

THOUGH THE DOOR WAS SOLID, I SWORE I COULD HEAR the boots of the soldiers, and I shivered again. It was Thomas himself who'd said King Damir didn't want a war, that he wouldn't move on Meirdre until Laurent was dead and our people amenable to foreign rule. Had he become impatient? Did he believe Laurent had turned weak in the wake of his bout with the measles? Had he found out about the payments Laurent was making to Iraela and believed he could manipulate Laurent just as easily?

"I am sorry for what I accused you of," Laurent continued, apparently unconcerned by my fears of an invasion. "I was a fool to even think it, much less treat you like—well, like I did. I was emotional. And I listened to the wrong people, people who don't know you and don't know our history. That won't happen again. Please believe me."

"I won't lie." I began to pace in a circle around the octagon. "That forgiveness you seek? It's further away now than it was."

He held out his hand as I stopped a suitable distance away. I bit my lip and looked up, unsure of what he wanted from me. Before, I'd knelt and kissed the back of his hand, but something told me that kind of formality was the last thing on his mind right now.

"Come here."

I stepped toward him, then stopped.

"You've been spending so much time dancing in that ballroom," he added, his voice rough. "And because of my foolish pride, I haven't been able to partake in your new skills. Before what's coming makes its way to Lochfeld . . . I'd like to."

Dance? Not the map? He wanted to dance with me here? Cautiously, I took his hand, and he pulled me toward him, his other hand sliding to my waist. My heart skipped a beat as it did, but before I could dwell on the consequences of that feeling, Laurent was dancing, sweeping me along with him in precise and sensuous motion. The stone floor of the war room wasn't the smooth mahogany of the ballroom, but I followed his lead as if it were. At that very moment, I would have danced with him anywhere. My brain screamed at me to walk away, but my soul . . . my soul wouldn't let me.

"I should have done this a long time ago," he whispered in my ear as we circled the table for the third time. "You deserved it—and so much more."

Too broken to resist whatever warped sense of kindness he'd finally managed to conjure up, I lay my head against his chest. The formality of the waltz was shattered then. One of his hands drew me against him, the other sat gently on the back of my head as I sobbed.

"I never wanted to make you unhappy." He whispered the claim in my ear, sending goosebumps shooting down my arms. "Ever. Please believe me."

"You did a fine job of it," I murmured against his chest. He wasn't getting away with that kind of tepid apology, not now. "More than once."

"I know I did. And fool that I am, I'll probably make you unhappy again." He wiped my tears with his thumb. "Though, in less severe means from now on—by snoring in your ear, perhaps. Or not praising your newest gown enough. Do you think you could love me anyway?"

Maybe we were both fools, because I didn't hesitate that time.

"As long as you keep trying."

I wanted to dance with him again, but a lamp flickered out, and we both turned toward it. The new darkness sent waves of shadows across the battlefield map, and Laurent released me to relight the oil. Without him holding me, I felt cold, and alone, and silly. Who cared about love when an invasion was about to destroy everything? Was that—the possibility of his death—why I suddenly felt this way about him?

"I think you should leave Lochfeld," he said, as I stared at the figurines. Maybe they were enough proof. "Go to Iraela, perhaps. Damir can't reach you there, not with that army of Marius's, and my mother wouldn't be displeased to see you. Neither would Juliana." His tone was dry, but there was an underlying emotion I couldn't identify. Concern?

"I can't read the map there. If I stay here, I can tell you when war is imminent."

Well, that wasn't quite true. I could tell if something was happening on the border. Timing? Hardly.

"Does the map matter now?" Laurent began to pace around the center table, touching the heads of the two figurines west of Brannitz and north of the Illrus River which separated Meirdre from Vassian—then slid the man at Brannitz south, toward where the river curved. "Along with Wennink's freedom comes an invasion. It's only a matter of time. When the snowmelt subsides and the river is passable once more . . . that's when they'll make their move."

Only once you're dead. Hadn't Laurent realized being at the spring with me had probably saved his life? He seemed too caught up in his new strategy to appreciate that was the case.

I edged toward the table and studied the figurines. He'd moved so many from the border of Nantoise that I had to wonder if he remembered the skirmish near Vistel the night of our betrothal ball. But Laurent had spies throughout the kingdom, and probably outside Meirdre, too. He knew what he was doing—didn't he?

"Sire, I don't want to be the one to remind you, but an assassination attempt would come first, and—"

"Yes." His reply was curt, but then again, how could it not have been? I'd just reminded him of his unwelcome mortality. "But the army is here now, and I can take care of myself. Vassian will not take Lochfeld without encountering more resistance than they can possibly imagine."

"Yes, but—"

"Riette, dear"—Laurent's lips curled into a half smile—"are you worried about me?"

I scoffed. A very unladylike sound, true, but he had me figured out, and I didn't like it. I didn't like that I *was* worried about him, or that he knew it.

"As you said, sire," I replied, lifting my chin and

looking him straight in the eyes, "you can handle yourself. Please make sure you do."

"I thought as much." He grinned, but it immediately fell. "Willem's burial is this evening. I would like you by my side."

I wanted to hold him, to kiss his cheek, to bring Captain Willem back, to do anything to take away his pain, but I simply nodded.

"It would be an honor."

A warm breeze ruffled my skirts as I stood next to Laurent in Lochfeld's royal graveyard. Transporting Willem's body to his hometown was out of the question with Thomas out there somewhere, and as Laurent rightly pointed out, it would have been his own body in the cool ground otherwise. I'd never argue with that.

Father Gerritt finished his prayer and nodded to the undertaker. I flinched as the first dirt hit the casket, but neither Father Gerritt nor Laurent showed any indication they'd heard the finality of the sound. With a slight touch at my elbow, Laurent nodded me inside, then stopped me next to an alcove.

"I want you to know," he began, "that—"

"Sire!" A shout interrupted him, followed by the dash

of boots on the marble floor. "There's a rider approaching. Perhaps another hour at his current speed. We'll have to be fast."

Laurent moved to push me farther into the alcove, but he was wasting his energy. I was already hiding from the commotion approaching us, the stone cold even through my clothing.

"Your men are prepared?" he asked.

The soldier handed over a sword. "Waiting on your word, sire."

I tried to slide around Laurent and the group of men who'd gathered, but Laurent slid the sword into his scabbard and nodded at me.

"Go with the lieutenant," he said, smoothing his sleeves. "He'll make sure you're safe."

"From one rider, I should hope so!" I'd never crossed Laurent, especially in front of anyone else, but my nerves were raw.

"Just go with him," he said through gritted teeth. "I have to see to this."

"You think it's Thomas?" Suddenly, a single rider seemed more of a threat than it did thirty seconds ago.

"It could be." Laurent's hand caressed the pommel of his sword. "And if it is, he won't be alone—this is a diversion if it's anything. But he's expecting a decimated royal guard, not a full company of soldiers. He'll be sorely disappointed when he finds out how well-guarded Lochfeld is now."

My heart thumped. Going with this soldier I'd never met before seemed the best idea. The safest. If Thomas had already returned, bringing an army of his own, I couldn't be found standing just inside a door that led outdoors. Still . . .

"I'd rather stay with you, sire. Please."

"I'd rather have the same thing. But this isn't your battle, and I need you safe. Please don't distract me by insisting otherwise."

I drew myself up. "Protecting Meirdre is my battle. If I can't stay with you—" I glanced around at the soldiers, then turned sideways and spoke under my breath. "Let me at least visit the ballroom first. I want to . . . check on things."

"Do you know something?" he asked. I shook my head, but Laurent's stance relaxed anyway. "Yes. Go. But they're going to accompany you, and the first sign something's wrong, you head to the keep."

"Agreed." I'd seen something happening to Lochfeld after all, but was this it? A single rider?

He nodded, kissed my hand, then disappeared into a throng of men, leaving me standing in the alcove. Able to breathe at last, I shook off the two soldiers at my sides and darted toward the ballroom with them at my heels. The room's oil lamps had been extinguished in preparation for an attack, but that would only make it easier for the map to speak to me.

Which it wasn't doing.

The space was dark, cold, and empty as I tiptoed inside. I couldn't see any of the inlays, so shrouded was the floor in shadows. That was good, wasn't it? But I'd seen the blue and gold sparkles over Lochfeld before. Why hadn't I finished Silke's journals when I had the chance? The answer didn't necessarily lie there, but if it was anywhere, it was in the writings of a woman who'd been a crownkeeper for much longer than myself.

"Your Grace, really," one of the men behind me said. "You must get somewhere safe."

I sighed.

"My room," I said. "Take me to my room."

One of the soldiers waited in the doorway while the other paced in circles around my room. Sara waited, wide-eyed, as I dug through the papers. It would have been easier to have her help, but she didn't know the secret of the map, and I wasn't going to be the one to tell her—though after I'd made such a fuss about seeing the journals tonight, Father Gerritt was going to have to lock them up again once I finished.

"Your Grace, I'm not sure . . ."

Her protests disappeared as I flung myself in a chair and skimmed Silke's later writings. Complaints about summer's ice storage failing. Fears of her children never growing up. Wonders about how much it'd snowed, this close to the coast.

Nothing about the map.

How was that possible? I had a chart of colors and disasters, though it hadn't meant anything up until now. Didn't this ancestor of Laurent's, who appeared much more skilled at her responsibility as crownkeeper than I, have something similar?

Maybe she didn't need a chart. Maybe the answer was so obvious she didn't even bother writing about it.

It was a disheartening thought. I flipped faster, looking for any mentions of blue sparkles.

Blue sky, blue silk, the blue of the ocean in the fall. Silke *really* liked to write about blue things.

Not helpful.

A shadow crossed my vision, and I looked up at the soldier who'd blocked the illumination of the one oil lamp allowed in the room.

"We need to leave, Your Grace. Now."

I blew out a deep breath and held up a hand. "Five more minutes."

He threw his hands in the air in reply, and I went back to the journal.

The floods in the Illrus river valley have been ghastly this spring. Dozens of Meirdreans dead already, so many crops lost. I suppose, if the pattern follows, that must have been why the map was blue a few months ago. A deep blue with gold sparkles, almost like the night sky. It's a relief to have my suspicions confirmed, but waiting months for the event the map predicts makes my soul uneasy. If I should see the same again, I'll take to my bed and not emerge until the crisis is over.

Shaky laughter escaped me.

I'd found it.

The colors had nothing to do with the type of crisis, even if my mind had been locked on the idea for months. They gave the crownkeeper—at least, one smart enough to figure it out—an idea of when they could expect trouble to occur. It seemed so obvious in hindsight, but I knew I'd have never figured it out without Silke's help.

But my relieved laughter had another cause—I hadn't seen anything lately besides the blue and gold, and if Silke was correct about the meaning, that meant the next attack on Meirdre was months away. I'd suspected nothing would happen until after the spring thaw and, heaven forbid, Laurent's death, but Silke had just confirmed it for me. How many months, I couldn't exactly predict, but that didn't matter now. For the moment, Lochfeld was safe, and I could say that with near certainty. Elation filled me, and then something akin to resignation, though much more joyful.

I could become a capable crownkeeper, invaluable to my people—if I so chose.

But right now there were soldiers on the ramparts above me, ready to fire on the rider approaching Lochfeld. The rider who was no threat. Not to Meirdre, at least, and Laurent *was* Meirdre. Though there was no doubt an attempt on his life was coming, this particular event was no assassination attempt. The map would have shown it, otherwise—and it had only called to me once when I'd missed it. That had been Thomas's rescue and Willem's murder, no doubt.

I sprang to my feet and darted past Sara and the soldiers. The latter ran after me, right on my heels, but none of the men would risk grabbing me. I was out of breath by the time I found the stairwell leading up to the rampart where I was sure Laurent had gone, and the threats from the soldiers had become a little louder and harsher, but I wouldn't let them kill an innocent person.

The night breeze ruffled my hair as I slowed my dash

to tiptoe along the wall, behind the musketeers and crossbowmen who scarcely moved at my presence. I couldn't imagine being that well-trained—or silent—for anything, especially an impending attack. I could see Laurent's figure through the shadows, just around the corner. The soldiers must have given up on stopping me, because I stormed up to him without being stopped. He swiveled toward me, shock and annoyance on his face, but I spoke before he could say anything.

"Sire, it's not Thomas coming." Laurent narrowed his eyes at me, and I hurried on, all too sure he'd send me back downstairs if he had half the chance. "I can't tell you how I know. Not right here and now. But this isn't an invasion, and it's not an assassination. Please, you can't fire on that rider!"

Laurent spun away from me instead of replying. "Who let her up here?" he hollered toward no one in particular. No one seemed to come to his rescue, and he took a step toward me.

"What do you really want? You know you shouldn't be up here, Riette. It's not safe, and I won't have it."

"Sire, please—I don't know who it is, and you know I can't tell you why. I'm just saying, please make entirely sure who you're shooting at!"

He folded his arms. "Well, if it's not the prelude to an invasion, what is it?" he asked, as my ineffectual guards finally caught up. "You can't just barge up here and tell me this without giving me some sort of information."

"I don't know." I shrugged. "I wish I could tell you more, but I can't."

Bad idea . . .

"Wait a minute, sire." The soldier next to Laurent lowered his spyglass and frowned at us both. "Unless you think Thomas Wennink sent a woman of, uh, advanced years, to do his work, I'd say that this isn't an attack."

CHAPTER FOURTEEN

THE AGING WOMAN, AS THE SOLDIER HAD REFERRED TO her, alternated her glare between Laurent and me as we stood in the gallery off the ballroom like children caught stealing milk from cold storage. I could tell Laurent would have rather been subjected to our reprimand in the comfortable formality of the throne room—where he could exert a little more control over the situation— but I also knew it would be a long time before he could set foot inside again. I simply wanted to flee before my part in the situation came to light, but Laurent had made it clear hiding wasn't an option. I'd turned into his protection, somehow.

"You almost killed me," the dowager queen said. "Your own mother!"

Laurent cleared his throat. "There was—"

"I don't care if you thought I had an entire army behind me! What were you thinking, preparing to fire at an unknown target? Of all the stupid, reckless ideas!"

"You were on a horse. By yourself. Not a carriage, not with a—"

"It's been forever on the road since Iraela, no servants, no guards. I left that sorry team and carriage in Haszen and borrowed a horse to make it the rest of the way. I didn't expect to be greeted by half an army waiting to take off my head!"

I shifted as Elsanne's tone grew more and more strident as her protests wore on. There was only one reason she was here, away from the control of her new husband, and when Laurent found out what I'd done, he would—

Oh, heavens, I didn't want to know what he'd do. I tried to slink backward, but Laurent took a breath and straightened, grabbing me by the wrist at the same time.

"You forget your place, Mother," he said, transforming from a scolded child into the king of Meirdre once more. "You are always welcome at Lochfeld, but while you are here, you will treat me with the respect I am entitled to."

Elsanne blinked at him. I turned toward him and

stared, though even as I did, I doubted the intelligence of questioning his authority, however subtly.

"Now"—having suitably frozen me with his reprimand, he let go of my wrist, though he didn't flinch at our reactions—"why don't we start over? Properly, if you would."

Elsanne swallowed, and I could tell she was debating how far to push him. I knew, because it was probably the same look I usually had on my face when I spoke with him in private.

"If you so insist, sire." Her annoyance turned swiftly to pride, and she dropped into a small curtsy. "It is so wonderful to see you again. It's been altogether too long."

Laurent glanced at me, like he expected me to intervene for some reason, but I stood motionless, my eyes flickering between the two of them. "It certainly is an honor to see you back at Lochfeld, Mother," he replied. "It has been a long time. May I ask what the occasion is?"

"You may not." Elsanne turned toward me, and even though she smelled like horse and I was properly attired and coiffed for a funeral, I felt like I was an inch tall. "You can ask your wife, if you're so curious."

Laurent didn't just glance at me that time. He turned

and faced me, his brows raised. "Riette, dear? What in the heavens is my mother talking about?"

"She . . ." I sank to the stone bench behind me, heedless of how the motion would offend either of them. "I don't know."

"Of course you do." Elsanne pulled a piece of paper from somewhere in her skirts and stuck it in Laurent's face. "She wrote me a letter, Laurent."

"A letter." Laurent glanced from the paper in his hand to me.

"A rather fascinating one in which she informed me that Marius is holding me hostage."

"Hostage. I—I see." Laurent had gone pale—with rage, I suspected. And that rage was likely not directed at his mother. It probably wasn't even directed at the king of Iraela.

"Well?" She fluttered it in front of him. "Are you going to do something about it?"

"Do—do something?"

Beginning to wonder if he'd developed a permanent stutter, I looked up.

"Your wife has overstepped her boundaries, and I won't stand for it!"

"She . . . ah . . . that's what you're upset about?"

"I love Marius. And don't give me that look," she said,

as Laurent grimaced and I glanced at the floor. "You've known that for a long time."

"Mother, it doesn't matter how you feel about him. He doesn't love you. I don't know what Riette told you in the letter, but the plain truth is, not only has he threatened to kill you if I don't keep paying him, but he has threatened to invade Meirdre! He's been blackmailing me since before you were married, Mother, and I've been paying him. It was a terrible idea, but I couldn't find a way out. But I will. I promise I will."

"Sire, if I could—" I began.

With a huff, Elsanne ignored me. "Do not presume to tell me what my husband feels for me."

"Mother, he might love you, but he loves the money I send more. I don't know what Riette told you, but—but she was probably right. She usually is. Well, always, actually."

Always? Had he finally lost his mind? Or his memory, at the very least? Or had he, at long last, truly admitted to himself that I'd had no involvement in Thomas's first attempt to overthrow the king?

What if everything he'd said in the clearing that day had been true?

"But you tried to sell me out for the protection of the kingdom? And you thought I'd never find out? I should think you'd know better than that."

I stood, too caught up in the possibility of an actual future with him to think rationally. "Sire, I—"

"We'll discuss *your* part in this later." His expression turned soft, for just a moment, then he folded his arms and turned back to his mother. "I made a mistake, Mother. And I will set it right, even if it means I have to protect Meirdre from an attack on both sides."

"You won't do anything of the sort." Elsanne snatched the letter back, shoved it back from wherever she'd produced it, and gave him a sly smile. "And you've already proven to me that you can't handle the situation, so I'm taking you out of it."

"He will kill you if you challenge him," Laurent ground out. "I will not allow that."

"Hardly. You'll forgive me, darling, if I don't trust your judgment about such things any longer. Now, if you don't mind, I need to make my way back to Iraela and discuss this new information with my husband. I'm sure with time and dialog that the three of us can come to a mutually beneficial agreement. One which needn't include you sending half your coinage outside of the kingdom." She glanced around, evidently at the almost-empty castle. "Heaven knows Lochfeld could use it."

Laurent's mouth fell open. "You cannot leave Lochfeld! Not in the middle of the night. Not for that man. You are not returning to Iraela now. Or ever. I forbid it, do you understand?"

"Forbid it?" Elsanne took a step forward, kissed his cheek, and laughed. "Dear boy, if Marius doesn't have the power over me that he thinks he does, what makes you think you do?"

"I have every authority over you." Laurent squared his shoulders. "You are still Meirdrean."

"Not," she replied, "since I married Marius."

His lips curled upward in a broad grin that was completely out of place in the conversation. I slid a little closer, as though my presence would cure him of the madness which seemed to have overtaken him.

"You think the left-handed marriage was his idea, didn't you?" he asked lightly.

"Of course." Elsanne blinked in confusion. "And I was happy to marry him all the same, even under that condition."

My breath caught.

Laurent wasn't as naïve as I'd thought, no, not even close. He'd succumbed to the king of Iraela's blackmail, yes, but he'd given Elsanne protection in the form of the only thing he could— recognition that as long as her marriage remained uneven, she remained a Meirdrean subject. Had even King Marius realized the drawback of the deal he'd made?

"Well, it wasn't his. It was mine." Then, brushing his fingertips against mine, he shouted down the corridor. "Lieutenant!"

Elsanne's eyes grew wide as the nearest soldier hurried toward us, questions in his own. I simply stared, the sensation of his touch hanging about me like a cloud. Laurent was standing up to her? He was siding with me? He—he had manipulated the king of Iraela like this?

"Find my mother a suitable suite for the next few weeks," he told the lieutenant. "And I want someone outside her to door to make sure she's safe."

"You're locking me in?" she all but screeched at him.

"Not exactly." Laurent's easy smile didn't falter. "But in case you hadn't noticed, Mother, war is on the horizon. What kind of a king—or son—would I be if I let harm come to you?"

The corridor fell silent except for the muted conversations of soldiers and servants somewhere in the distance. Laurent's fingertips found mine once more, and my heart thumped wildly as I pressed my lips closed and waited for Elsanne's reply.

"And what of Juliana?" she demanded.

"What of her?" He ran his thumb across the palm of my hand, and I sucked in a breath. "If Marius loves you as much as you claim, he'd dare not hurt her. Or were you misleading me about his feelings for you? Speak carefully—I do hate being lied to."

Her jaw dropped, as if she couldn't believe he'd reprimanded her, then she lifted her chin.

"She'll be fine."

"Good. Then we can carry out a friendly exchange sometime in the future, yes?"

"If you so will it, sire." She tossed her hair and turned to the lieutenant. "I have my own rooms. You may follow me."

And then, without even a curtsy or nod in Laurent's direction, she disappeared.

The soldiers still patrolled the corridors when I finally made my way to my room, but Sara was more than happy to act like nothing untoward had happened today, or even the past week, for that matter. Nothing was said of Thomas's escape, nor of the soldiers outside, nor of Elsanne's unexpected visit.

"They say the spring rains will end soon," she said, pulling a chemise over my head. "It will be a nice change from this dreary weather, don't you think?"

I didn't think. Lack of rains plus the end of the

snowmelt floods meant the armies of Vassian could cross the river.

"Yes," I lied, praying she'd finish quickly and go away. "It will be nice to see the sun."

"You have been looking a bit pale. I think—"

A knock sounded on the door, interrupting what she thought I needed. Sara rushed to open it, only to reveal Laurent standing there. I couldn't tell which one of us was more surprised to see him. Probably me, since Sara curtsied and hurried out in the same amount of time it took me to stand.

"I didn't want to interrupt," he said, closing the door.

"You didn't." I glanced at the fireplace. A single ember glowed, and for some reason, I felt as though I'd failed in preparing for his unexpected visit. "Though I should have had her relight the fire."

"No need." Laurent strode quickly across my room and knelt before the hearth to fan the flames back to life. "This is my duty, not hers."

His? In his entire life, had Laurent ever lit his own fire? I wanted to laugh at the stark inaccuracy of his comment, but after the fire caught and he stood and turned toward me, his expression was somber.

"We ought to discuss the letter," he said.

"I will not apologize for that." My bravery, reckless as

it was, surprised me, though it didn't look like I'd surprised Laurent. "Ever."

"I didn't expect you would." He rubbed the back of his neck, a startlingly vulnerable movement. "And I would never ask it of you. I'm beginning to understand that it would be a waste of breath, anyway."

"I had only good intentions. She had to know. What you subjected her to was unfair, and very unlike you, sire."

In fact, it was exactly like the Laurent I'd first met, but what had Father Gerritt once said about tipping the sum of Laurent's works toward good? He was responsible for that outrageous agreement with Iraela, but my cautious lie could easily tip him in the opposite direction, especially if he thought changing his mind was his own idea.

"And she may well work herself out of the predicament I put her in. I do worry more about Marius than her." Laurent sighed and fell onto my settee by the window. "And yet, I cannot have you undermining my authority in that matter or any other."

My entire body grew hot, and it wasn't from the flames. Why had he restarted the fire if he was going to lecture me? Or worse—punish me like he'd ordered before? We couldn't keep starting over time after time. If he wanted me to forgive him, then we needed to move on. As husband and wife.

"I never meant—" I began.

"You think this is about my ego, don't you?" He sprawled then, an arm draped over the back of the seat, and I frowned at his casualness. "I wouldn't blame you for thinking that, though you'd be wrong."

"How so?"

He grinned, an odd reaction for such a serious conversation. "You will be in charge of Lochfeld when I leave for the Vassian border."

"What?" The question spilled out in a frantic rush as I dashed toward him. He stood, stopping me in his arms. "You can't do that," I said to his shoulder. "You know what will happen."

"Your flattering concern for me is duly noted, Riette." He tilted my chin upward, and his tone grew grim. "They must not be allowed to take the heart of Meirdre. Our access to the coast. Never. We will meet them in the south and prevent that."

"And what if you don't?" I whispered. "What if—"

"They kill me first?" Laurent kissed my forehead and then my cheek. "Then I suppose I shall die thinking of you."

My knees went weak. "How can you joke about this?"

"It's either joke about it or fall apart." He leaned his

cheek against mine. "And what would Meirdre think of me if that happened?"

"That was rhetorical," I replied with no small amount of acerbity. "And another inappropriate joke."

"Well, now you have an answer to a question that would have bothered you until I left." He backed toward the settee, dragging me along by the hands, then collapsed with a laugh, pulling me onto his lap. I let out a yelp as I fell, and he drew me against him, his mouth against my ear. "And now I need an answer from you."

"Yes," I stammered. "I'll protect Lochfeld. As I was meant to. Even if—even if it means I never leave the castle grounds again." My stomach flipped a bit at my vow, but Laurent's touch drove away any remaining indecision. He needed me, not for him, not for Meirdre, but for both. I'd always felt it, but now there was a certain amount of power in *knowing*.

"If that's the sacrifice you feel you need to make, then I'll make certain it's not in vain. I swear to you." A hand drifted downward, resting on the small of my back. "But I wasn't speaking of the map, Riette."

His lips crept down my jaw, lingering at the corner of my own. I closed my eyes, too afraid of what I was about to do—and much too desperate. Laurent's hand found a smattering of hair pins as I clung to him, achingly incomplete, and by the time I pulled away to gasp for air, my hair was undone, his tunic askew.

"Now, no more talk of war," he said, his voice thick. "We've other things to sort out right now."

"For how long?" I asked his neck. War was coming, and I needed to know how long I had with the man I was falling in love with.

"Hmm. Let's say for tonight, for a start. And after that?" He leaned back and studied me, his eyes sparkling like I'd never seen before. "As long as you'll have me."

ACKNOWLEDGMENTS

Once again, I couldn't have done it without Meghan, Cathy, and Ed. Also a huge thanks to everyone who read *Treason's Crown* and asked for more. You are the reason this book exists.

ABOUT THE AUTHOR

Anne Wheeler grew up with her nose in a book but earned two degrees in aviation before it occurred to her she was allowed to write her own. When not working, moving, or writing her next novel, she can be found planning her next escape to the desert—camera gear included. She currently lives in Georgia with her husband, son, and herd of cats.

For more information:
www.anne-wheeler.com